GREATER THAN RICHES

BY
JENNIFER TAYLOR

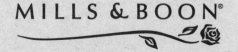

MILLS & BOON®

*First published in Great Britain 2000
Harlequin Mills & Boon Limited,
Eton House, 18-24 Paradise Road, Richmond, Surrey TW9 1SR*

© Jennifer Taylor 2000

ISBN 0 263 82249 4

*Set in Times Roman 10 on 11½ pt.
03-0007-61986*

*Printed and bound in Spain
by Litografia Rosés, S.A., Barcelona*

Jennifer Taylor has been writing Mills & Boon® romances for some time, but only recently discovered Medical Romances™. She was so captivated by these heart-warming stories that she immediately set out to write them herself! As a former librarian who worked in scientific and industrial research, Jennifer enjoys the research involved with the writing of each book as well as the chance it gives her to create a cast of wonderful new characters. When not writing or doing research for her latest book, Jennifer's hobbies include reading, travel, and walking her dog. She lives in the north-west of England with her husband and children.

Recent titles by the same author:

TENDER LOVING CARE
THE HUSBAND SHE NEEDS*
HOME AT LAST*

A Country Practice

'Does that mean what I think it does?' Stephen asked blandly.

A touch of colour bloomed in Alex Campbell's face. 'Graham has been kind enough to let me stay at the house since I started working here. I believe you are going to be staying here as well while you're covering for him.' Her lids shot up as she looked him squarely in the eyes. 'It appears that we are going to be housemates for the next six weeks. I do hope that isn't going to be a problem for you, Dr Spencer.'

CHAPTER ONE

'IF THERE was another solution, Stephen, I wouldn't ask. I know I'm putting you on the spot but I have no choice. My consultant has told me that I cannot delay having this operation any longer. It's now or never basically.'

'You're a damned fool to have waited this long, Graham.' Dr Stephen Spencer got up from his desk and went to the window, impatience etched in every tense line of his powerful body. He barely saw the leafy avenue of trees outside the surgery gates as his mind raced with what he had just heard. He swung round and his dark grey eyes were full of concern as they rested on his old friend and mentor, Graham Barker.

'It's your life on the line here, Graham, dammit! I know you'd had some trouble a while back...mild angina was what you told me, nothing to worry about. Every time I've asked how you were since then you've passed it off. You certainly never mentioned that it had got bad enough to warrant bypass surgery!'

Graham looked uncomfortable. 'There didn't seem any point in worrying you. The drugs I was on were fine at first but things have got steadily worse and surgery is now my best option. I was hoping to get a locum in to cover for me while I'm in hospital, but I haven't had any luck finding anyone.'

'I can understand that.' Stephen sighed as he sat down again behind the elegant mahogany desk. A wry smile suddenly softened the austerely handsome lines of his face. 'Let's face it, working in your practice isn't exactly a picnic! It's one of the toughest areas of the city and not many people would willingly opt to do even a short stint there, I imagine.'

'Exactly. I've been on to several of the biggest agencies *and* run an ad in the *BMJ*, but so far no one's applied for the post. I doubt I'll get anyone either, to be honest. The number of young doctors opting for general practice is dropping all the time, and who can blame them for not wanting to cut their teeth on a post like this?' Graham sighed heavily. 'It's you or nobody, Stephen—that's what it boils down to.'

'I see.' Stephen ran a hand through his immaculately groomed fair hair. Tilting the big leather chair back, he stared around the expensively furnished consulting room. He had worked long and hard to get where he was today, but if it hadn't been for Graham, believing in him, he would never have got a toe on the first rung of the ladder. It wasn't that hard to decide what he should do.

'How long would you need me for? Obviously, I'd have to make provision here for me being away, but it won't be anywhere near as difficult for me to find cover. Miles and I have a list of people willing to locum for us,' he added dryly.

'I can imagine! Working in a place like this, that must be a dream come true for most doctors.' Graham smiled but it only served to emphasise how worn-out he looked. Stephen did some rapid mental arithmetic and realised with a shock that Graham had to be almost sixty now. He ran the figures through his head once more but there was no mistake. He was thirty-five, which meant that Graham was fifty-nine, with a birthday coming up in a few months' time. How the years had flown by!

'Anyway, I'd need you for six weeks maximum. Simon Ross—that's my consultant—has said that I should be fit enough to go back to work after six weeks. Alex has postponed her holidays until it's all over, bless her, so she'll be there the whole time you'll be covering for me. That should ease things a lot.'

'Alex?' Stephen frowned at the unfamiliar name.

'Alex Campbell. Of course, you haven't met her, have you? She started about six months ago and she's been a real godsend.

I never thought I'd find anyone suitable after Peter decided he'd had enough and moved to the suburbs. I must say that I was dubious about taking Alex on—you'll understand why when you see her,' he added in a laughing aside. 'But, to be frank, I doubt I could have found anyone better. She's been brilliant!'

Stephen smiled thinly, somewhat surprised by this lavish testament. He couldn't recall Graham being this fulsome before about any of the long line of junior doctors who had passed through his practice. It made him wonder what this Alex Campbell had which deserved such unstinting praise.

'I shall look forward to meeting her, then. Now, when exactly do you need me to start? Have you got a definite date for the operation yet?' he asked, pushing the thought to the back of his mind while he dealt with practicalities.

'It's been left open. Simon Ross told me to contact him as soon as I'd managed to arrange things my end.' Graham sounded sheepish. 'I've been on the top of his list for months now but I've kept holding my name back because of the problem of finding someone to cover for me.'

Stephen sighed heavily. 'You're a fool, Graham. You aren't doing yourself or your patients any good by taking such a risk with your health.' He cut short the rest of the lecture, knowing that all his life Graham had put others first. 'Anyway, shall we say the beginning of next week? Can you clear things with Ross that quickly?'

'No problem. But are you sure you can get away at such short notice, Stephen?' Graham asked with a frown. 'I don't want to make things difficult for you here.'

'I have some time owing to me and I was planning on taking it then,' Stephen explained, carefully omitting to mention that he also had a holiday booked. Three weeks' sailing around the Greek islands on a yacht he'd chartered with a group of friends, to be precise. Maybe he should have felt disappointed at the thought of missing the trip but it didn't worry him a bit.

He frowned as he realised that the lure of exotic holidays

had started to pall some while back. Even when he'd gone skiing in the Andes at Christmas, it had been purely because it would have disrupted everyone else's plans if he'd pulled out. Oh, he'd enjoyed the fresh air and exercise but it hadn't left him longing to go again, as it used to do. In fact, if he was being honest, it had been ages since he'd looked forward to *anything* very much. It was as though everything he had striven so hard for was suddenly meaningless.

He pushed that disquieting thought to the back of his mind as Graham stood up, preferring not to think any more about it right then.

'Then all I can say is thank you, Stephen. I really appreciate this. As I said before, I wouldn't have asked—'

'Look, Graham, you can get it right out of your head that I'm doing you a huge favour.' Stephen stood up as well and came round the desk to clap the older man on the shoulder in a show of affection which would have surprised his friends. He wasn't a demonstrative man by nature, having learned early in his life to hide his feelings, but he and Graham went back a long way, to a past which few people knew about. 'I'm only too pleased to be able to help out, believe me!'

'Let's hope you still feel like that at the end of your tenure,' Graham joked. 'You'll probably be sorry you offered! Still, it's a big weight off my mind, knowing that I'm leaving the place in such capable hands. And Alex will be thrilled as well. I've told her such a lot about you, Stephen. She's dying to meet you.'

'And I'm looking forward to meeting her, as I said.' Stephen tried to inject some enthusiasm into his voice but he could hear the flat note it held even if Graham didn't appear to notice it. Already he was wondering what it was going to be like, working with such a paragon.

He tried to picture her as he walked Graham to the door, conjuring up an immediate picture of some earnest-looking woman, rather plain and sturdy, someone capable of dealing with the often volatile situations encountered in a practice in the heart of the city.

He sighed as he saw Graham out. Undoubtedly, Alex Campbell was a gem but he couldn't imagine they would have much in common. It could turn out to be a very long six weeks indeed!

A summer thunderstorm darkened the city streets, making them look even more dreary as Stephen drove to Graham's house the following Monday. It had been years since he had been in this part of the city yet he felt no affection for the area where he had grown up. It held too many bad memories to allow for any feelings of nostalgia.

He turned in through the rusting iron gates and drew up in front of the surgery, which was tagged onto the side of the house. It was well after seven but the lights were still on inside and there were a number of people sitting in the waiting-room when he went in.

Stephen tried not to compare the drab, cream-painted walls and functional black plastic chairs with the understated luxury of the comparable area in his own surgery, but it was hard not to when it was such a sharp reminder of the differences between the two practices. It made him feel a bit uncomfortable, although he wasn't sure why that should be.

He hurriedly dismissed the feeling as he went to the desk and discovered that Dorothy was still working behind it. She didn't look round at first, busily scribbling a note on the pad beside the telephone as she spoke over her shoulder.

'Surgery ended half an hour ago, but if it's really urgent Dr Campbell will probably squeeze you in if you want to wait.'

'Oh, I don't think I need to see a doctor, thanks all the same. Just seeing you again is tonic enough,' he replied, laughing as he saw the surprise on her face as she spun round.

'Stephen! What are you doing here?' Her face broke into a

broad smile as she hurried towards him. 'Oh, but never mind that. Come here!'

She leaned across the counter and hugged him, unconcerned by the interested glances being shot their way. Stephen laughed as he planted a kiss on her lined cheek.

'It's lovely to see you, Dorothy. How are you?' he asked, drawing back to run his gaze from the top of her dyed black hair down over the gaudy pink blouse she was wearing with a short yellow skirt. It was only a guess because Dorothy had always refused to divulge her age to anyone, but she must have turned seventy by his estimation, not that she ever allowed age to deter her from wearing whatever took her fancy!

He grinned wickedly at her. 'I don't think you need to answer that. I can see for myself that you're looking even more beautiful than ever!'

'Oh, get on with you,' she chided, but he could see that she was delighted by the compliment all the same. 'Dr Barker said that you'd be coming but I thought he was having me on, to be honest. It's been so long since you visited us last, Stephen, that I thought you'd forgotten how to get here!'

He grimaced at the rebuke, knowing in his heart that it was justified. He always tried to avoid coming to the surgery to see Graham, preferring to meet him in town for lunch, although, now that he thought about it, he realised that it had been a while since Graham had accepted an invitation.

Graham had claimed that he'd been too busy each time Stephen had rung him recently, although probably the real truth was that Graham had known that Stephen would have immediately suspected how ill he'd been if they'd met.

He felt suddenly angry with himself for letting his old friend pull the wool over his eyes like that. He should have realised there was something wrong long before now!

'I've no excuse, Dorothy. I only wish…' he began, then broke off as a woman suddenly appeared through the door leading from the office. She was holding a file in her hand, a deep frown marring her brow as she stared at what was written on it, but even that couldn't detract from her beauty.

Stephen felt his heart give a small jolt as he took rapid stock of the dark red hair drawn into a coil at the nape of her elegant neck, the porcelain-fine complexion, the cameo-like profile. That was all he could see because her head was still bent as she concentrated on what was written in the notes. She suddenly looked up and he felt his heart come to a complete stop this time as he got his first really good look at her.

She was exquisite! That was the only word to describe her, although he wasn't a man given to extremes normally. Yet he doubted that he had ever seen anyone as lovely in the whole of his life.

With an urgency he couldn't explain, his gaze took in the softly rounded chin, the ripe curve of her lips, the sculpted cheek-bones. He wasn't aware of it but he was actually holding his breath, afraid that something…no matter how small…would spoil the picture of perfection.

His eyes finally connected with a pair of heavily lashed sea-green ones and he felt another bolt of shock rip through him as he saw the chilly dislike they held. It stunned him. What on earth had he done to earn himself such a look of disapproval from this gorgeous creature?

'You must be Stephen Spencer. Graham said that you would be arriving tonight.'

Her voice was low but there was no denying the animosity it held and Stephen frowned. 'That's right. And you are…?'

'Alex Campbell.' She wasted no time on pleasantries, assuming that he would know who she was from that curt introduction. Her green eyes were even cooler as they skimmed from the top of his dark blond hair to the tips of his hand-made leather shoes, but nothing along the route seemed to warm the icy gleam they held.

Stephen felt the first stirrings of anger as her gaze returned to his face. He wasn't used to being scrutinised like that, and he certainly wasn't used to beautiful women finding him lacking…in any area! But there was no disputing that Alex Campbell appeared less than impressed by what she had seen. It was an effort to concentrate when she spoke again.

'Graham was admitted to hospital early this morning. His consultant decided that even another night's delay would be too risky.' She glanced at the workmanlike watch strapped to her slender wrist and there was a husky note in her sweetly modulated voice as she continued. 'They should be operating this very minute, I imagine.'

'I see. I had no idea—' He broke off, realising how inane that sounded. If Graham had been postponing his operation for as long as Stephen suspected then it would be urgent by this stage.

He drew himself up to his full six feet two and stared at the woman before him. He couldn't explain it, but he had the feeling that Alex Campbell blamed him in some way for what had happened. Shrugging aside such a ridiculous notion, he concentrated instead on necessities. 'I take it that's why you still have so many patients waiting to be seen?'

Alex nodded, her luscious lips compressing as she glanced towards the waiting-room. She wasn't wearing a scrap of make-up, Stephen realised as his concentration wavered once more but, then, she didn't need any. It would have been like gilding a lily to add cosmetics to such perfection.

'Yes. We've been running behind all day. There was no way that we could cancel appointments—most of our patients aren't on the phone for starters. Dorothy managed to persuade a few non-urgent cases to come back later in the week, but these people need to see a doctor tonight rather than in a few days' time.' Her gaze came back to him as she finished speaking but it was just as cold as ever.

'I see. Then it's a pity that you didn't think to inform me of what had happened earlier, isn't it?' Stephen gave her a thin smile, determined not to let her see how her reaction had irked him. He had no idea why she should have taken a dislike to him but he had no intention of letting her know that it bothered him!

He swung round on his heel and headed for the door, pausing when she said sharply, 'Wait! Where are you going? You gave Graham your word…'

He stopped to look back, his mouth curving into a mocking smile which brought a touch of delicate colour to Alex Campbell's cheeks when she saw it. 'I never go back on my word, Dr Campbell. Rest assured of that. I promised Graham that I would cover for him and I intend to do just that, starting right now.'

He paused to let that sink in then glanced at Dorothy. 'Give me five minutes to find where everything is then send the first patient in, would you, Dorothy, please? I'll be in Dr Barker's consulting room.'

He left the waiting-room without another word and walked along the corridor to the largest of the two consulting rooms. He sat down behind the desk, smiling cynically as he recalled the surprise on the young doctor's face. It was obvious she hadn't expected him to do that and he was pleased that he had managed to disconcert her a little. She had certainly managed to disconcert him!

His smile faded abruptly as he thought about the chilly reception he'd received. It appeared that the beautiful Dr Campbell had built up her own picture of him, and that it hadn't been a flattering one either! Still, in all fairness, he couldn't blame her when he was guilty of much the same thing. So much for the earnest-looking professional of his imagination. Alex Campbell in the beautiful flesh was something entirely different!

He sighed as he opened the desk drawer and took out a prescription pad. He might have needed to make a rapid adjustment to the picture he had formed of her but he suspected it was going to take rather longer to change Alex Campbell's view of him. The thought bothered him, although he wasn't sure why it should. After all, they would be working together for only a few weeks so what difference did it make what she thought of him? It was very strange indeed.

'Right, Mrs Murphy, you can put Tommy's jumper back on now.'

Stephen went to the sink and carefully scrubbed his hands with disinfectant soap from the dispenser screwed to the wall. Rolling his shirtsleeves down, he slipped his jacket back on and sat down as Ellen Murphy finished pulling the sweatshirt over the six-year-old boy's head.

'What's wrong with him, Doctor? He's drivin' me mad, scratchin' all the time.' Mrs Murphy swatted the child's hand as young Tommy started scratching again almost before the words were out of her mouth. 'See what I mean?'

'I do, indeed.' Stephen smiled sympathetically at the little boy. 'I bet it's getting you down, isn't it, son?'

Tommy nodded mutely, surreptitiously using the toe of his trainer to deal with an itch on his leg. However, Ellen Murphy's hand shot out like lightning once again.

'Stop that! How many more times do I have to tell you?'

'It isn't really Tommy's fault, Mrs Murphy,' Stephen put in quickly, feeling sorry for the child. 'Tommy has scabies and the itching must be very irritating for him.'

'Scabies?' Ellen Murphy was momentarily distracted from doling out another slap. Stephen could tell that she had no real idea what scabies was so he quietly explained.

'It's a skin infestation caused by tiny mites…insects…which burrow under the skin and lay their eggs. If you look at Tommy's hands you can see those scaly grey swellings between his fingers. Those are the mite's burrows. The infestation causes an intense itching, which is why Tommy is constantly scratching. Unfortunately, that leads to the skin being damaged, which is what has caused all those sores,' he added, pointing to the scabs on the child's hands and forearms.

'Well, I don't know where he's got it from, that's for sure!' Ellen Murphy sounded indignant. 'If you're tryin' to say that my house is dirty then I'll have you know that you could eat your tea off my floor!'

'I wasn't implying any such thing, Mrs Murphy.' Stephen smiled disarmingly. 'Unfortunately, not everyone is as particular as you are and if Tommy has come into contact with someone who has scabies then that's how he's caught it.'

'Oh, I see. Well, that's different.' Ellen Murphy sniffed. 'There's plenty of folk round here who don't know one end of a scrubbin' brush from the other. Happen Tommy's caught it off those Richardson kids. House must be filthy, what with the mother out drinkin' from the time the pub opens of a mornin' to when it shuts at night. And as for the father... Well!'

She left the rest of the sentence unsaid and Stephen bit back a sigh. He didn't need to hear the rest of it. He knew only too well how so many people in the area lived. The contrast between the lifestyles of the patients he would see here and the ones who came to his own surgery couldn't have been more marked, so that he experienced a momentary qualm at what he had taken on. However, no matter how difficult he found it, he intended to do the job to the very best of his ability. It was the very least he could do for Graham.

'I'm going to give you a prescription for lindane to treat the infestation,' he explained to Ellen. 'The best way to deal with it is to give Tommy a bath then apply the lotion afterwards, making sure that you cover the whole of his body from the chin down. He'll need a second and a third application at twelve-hourly intervals, followed by another bath.

'Make sure he puts on clean underwear afterwards, and that his bedclothes are changed and put through a hot wash. Unfortunately, scabies is highly contagious so everyone in the household must be treated at the same time. Have you any other children, Mrs Murphy?'

'Five.' Ellen Murphy announced flatly. 'Looks as though I'm goin' to have a lot of extra washin', doesn't it?'

'I'm afraid so.' Stephen smiled sympathetically. 'And although I hate to add to your workload, don't forget that you and your husband are going to have to go through the same procedure, will you? The only way to make sure that you've got rid of scabies is by treating it in one fell swoop, I'm afraid.'

Ellen gave her son a baleful look as she took the prescription. 'Well, it's the last time you're playin' with the likes of the Richardsons, me lad! As if I haven't enough to do without all this…' She was still muttering as she left.

Stephen smiled ruefully to himself. He wouldn't want to be in young Tommy's shoes for the next few days!

It was well after eight by the time the last patient was sent on his way. Stephen gathered up the bundle of record cards and took them through to the office for filing. Dorothy was putting her coat on and she looked round as he went in.

'Leave them in the tray and I'll do them in the morning, Stephen. It's too late to bother now. My Rita will be wondering where I am as it is.'

'How is she?' he asked as he dropped the cards into the tray. Dorothy's daughter, Rita, now in her mid-forties, had developed scoliosis of the spine in her early teens, which, unfortunately, had gone untreated. In those days the signs hadn't been picked up on as quickly as they would have been now. Rita's spine was severely deformed as a consequence, her body twisted into the characteristic S-shape.

She and Dorothy lived in a council flat close to the surgery and Stephen had got to know her quite well. Despite her handicap, Rita was a very positive woman who enjoyed life and he had a great deal of admiration for her.

'She's fine. But you know our Rita, never lets anything get her down—' Dorothy broke off as someone came into the room behind him. Stephen didn't glance round because there was no need. There were only the three of them there so it had to be Alex Campbell. It didn't need a detective to work that out, especially not when he had already recognised the perfume she wore as it wafted towards him—Opium.

The realisation shook him. He took one of the files back out of the tray and pretended to read it while he tried to get a grip on himself. Exactly when had he stored away that snippet of information? He had no idea but it made him uncomfortable to realise that he had picked up on something so...so inconsequential!

'You look all in, love. No wonder, with the day you've had.' Dorothy turned her attention to the newcomer, mercifully giving Stephen a chance to get his thoughts together.

He pored over the file until he could have recited every detail from memory. He heard a footstep behind him but he still didn't look round, holding his breath so that he wouldn't get another lungful of scented air. His nerves were already shot, his skin prickling with awareness. He hadn't realised before just how potent that particular perfume was!

'Excuse me.' The quiet words couldn't be ignored, even though he was doing his best to ignore the woman who had uttered them. Stephen stepped aside with a murmured apology, his eyes never leaving the file—rubella in 1997, tonsillitis the same year... Tommy Murphy's medical history made fascinating reading to someone determined not to be sidetracked in any way!

'I'll leave these in the tray with the others, shall I, Dorothy?' Alex Campbell tossed a bundle of files into the appropriate receptacle with what seemed to Stephen to be a tad too much force. He frowned, wondering what had upset her, although he still didn't look up. Another minute and he should be feeling better able to cope, although he had no idea why he should be so edgy all of a sudden.

So he and the beautiful Dr Campbell had got off on the

wrong foot. Was that why he felt so keyed up, because he was still smarting from the chilly reception he had received? It was the only rational explanation he could come up with.

'Yes. I'll sort 'em out in the morning. I'm off home now to put me feet up. That's what you should do, love.' Dorothy gave a cackling laugh which gained Stephen's attention despite his determination not to be drawn into the conversation. 'Tell you what, why don't you get Stephen to do the cooking tonight? He used to be a dab hand with a frying-pan, so Dr Barker always said. Right, I'll be off then. See you both tomorrow. Ta-ta.'

Dorothy hurried on her way but for a few seconds after she'd left Stephen found himself incapable of movement. He took a deep breath as he ran back through what the elderly receptionist had said, trying not to believe what it seemed to imply...

Another bundle of cards landed in the tray with only slightly less force and he knew that he couldn't put off the inevitable any longer. He turned round, carefully wiping every vestige of expression from his face as his eyes met the challenge issuing from a pair of icy green ones.

'Does that mean what I think it does?' he asked blandly.

A touch of colour bloomed in Alex Campbell's face. Something which looked almost like panic glimmered in her eyes before she lowered her lids, yet when she spoke it was with a chilly composure that showed him what a fanciful notion that had been. Panic was a word he doubted the beautiful Dr Campbell knew how to spell!

'Graham has been kind enough to let me stay at the house since I started working here. It was more convenient, you understand.' She shrugged, seemingly oblivious to the mounting tension. Stephen could feel it, though, and he steeled himself not to show how he felt as she continued in the same enviably controlled manner.

'I believe you are going to be staying here as well while

you're covering for him.' Her lids shot up as she looked him squarely in the eyes. 'It appears that we are going to be house-mates for the next six weeks. I do hope that isn't going to be a problem for you, Dr Spencer.'

CHAPTER TWO

THE ensuing silence was deafening to Stephen's ears. He hurried to fill it, afraid that the lack of words might say rather more than he wanted it to.

'No, of course it isn't a problem. If you don't mind, neither do I.'

'Good. I'm sure that we—' Alex broke off as the phone rang. 'Excuse me. I'll just go and see who that is.'

She moved away and Stephen took a deep breath. It didn't make him feel any better unfortunately. Why in heaven's name hadn't Graham thought to mention that he would be sharing the house with Alex?

He sighed as he stared at the back of her bent head. Probably because Graham hadn't imagined it would be a problem. And, in all honesty, it shouldn't be. After all, they were two intelligent adults brought together by necessity if not by choice. Surely they were capable of handling the situation?

The fact that he wasn't wholly convinced of that worried him a bit but he pushed it to the back of his mind as he went out to his car to get his things. Alex was still on the phone when he passed the office on his way through to the house so he didn't stop.

He heard her laugh at something the person on the other end of the line said before he moved out of earshot. Letting himself into the house, he went straight upstairs, wondering to whom she was talking. It was obviously a personal call so probably a friend, but male or female?

Definitely male, he decided as he pushed open the bedroom door and tossed his case onto the bed. There had been something about the way she had laughed just now...

20

He swore softly as he realised what he was doing. What business was it of his to whom she was speaking? They might be colleagues and housemates for the next six weeks but that was as far as it went. He certainly didn't want to go prying into her private life any more than he wanted her prying into his!

He had almost finished unpacking when the sound of footsteps on the landing warned him that he was about to have company. He looked around as Alex appeared, wondering if it had been the chat with her 'friend' which had added an unaccustomed warmth to her expression. The thought irritated him a little, although he had no idea why it should, so that he rammed the shirts he was holding into a drawer with scant regard for the state they would be in when he came to wear them. Frankly, a few creases were the least of his worries!

'That was Simon Ross on the phone,' she informed him without any preamble. 'Graham has had the operation and everything went smoothly. They will be taking him down to ICU once he comes round from the anaesthetic.'

'That's great news.' Stephen forgot his irritation in an instant as he suddenly realised just how worried he had been about his old friend. 'Did Ross say when we can see him?'

'Simon wants to keep things as quiet as possible for the next twenty-four hours,' she informed him, coming into the room. 'He said that Graham can have visitors from Wednesday but that we're not to discuss work or anything that might worry him. He doesn't want Graham becoming at all stressed.'

'Understandable,' Stephen agreed, stowing the case on top of the old-fashioned wardrobe. He wasn't deaf to the easy familiarity with which she'd referred to the consultant, but it wasn't his place to question how well she knew Simon Ross, even though he would have dearly loved to have done so. Instead, he glanced round the room, latching onto the first thing which came to mind to stop himself giving in to curiosity.

'It's like walking into a time warp, coming back here. I

doubt if Graham has changed a thing for years. I'd swear those are the same curtains that were up when I lived here. I'll have to ask him when I go to visit him.'

'You lived here? For how long?' she shot back, sounding startled.

'Oh, quite some time. From when I was fourteen right up until I went to university, in fact.' He shrugged, faintly surprised that she hadn't known. 'Didn't Graham tell you?'

'No. He never mentioned it. Oh, he's spoken about you many times, but he never told me that you'd actually lived here with him.'

The chill was back with a vengeance, frosting each word, and Stephen frowned. What was the matter now? She was acting as though he had committed some sort of *crime* yet he had no idea what he could have done!

For a moment he debated asking her before it struck him that it might not be wise. Obviously, the news that he had lived in the house had come as a surprise, but did he really want to arouse her curiosity any further as to the reason why? He never discussed his past with anyone and it would have been foolish to have discussed it with Alex when it could have given her an even bigger stick to beat him with.

However, before he could think of a plausible way of avoiding any further questions, Alex took the momentum from him. 'Obviously, there's no need for me to give you the grand tour, then. You must know your way around better than I do. I'll leave you to get settled in, Dr Spencer.'

She gave him a last cool smile, icy even by her standards, then left the room. Stephen heard a door further along the landing close a few seconds later. He raised his eyes to the heavens and sighed in frustration.

He seemed to have a real knack for upsetting her, even though he wasn't sure what he had done this time! Or did he need to *do* anything other than be himself? The simple truth was that Alex seemed to have taken a dislike to him, although for the life of him he couldn't understand why. Had Graham said something which had coloured her view perhaps?

He dismissed that thought immediately. Graham would never have said anything derogatory about him. On the contrary, his old friend had always been embarrassingly proud of his achievements. No, Alex didn't like him and it was as simple as that. But, that being the case, it was going to be even more of a strain living here than he'd imagined!

The light was on in the kitchen when Stephen went downstairs a short time later. He hesitated but the hungry growling of his stomach wouldn't be ignored. Alex was propped against the worktop, flicking through a magazine and munching an apple. She didn't appear to have heard him so he took the opportunity to take rapid stock of what she was wearing, mainly because it was worth taking.

Jeans and the baggiest of baggy black T-shirts wouldn't have been his first choice for many women but she wore them well, he had to admit. His appreciative gaze roamed over the slender contours of her body while he felt the most unseemly reaction start to fizzle in the pit of his stomach.

He shifted abruptly to ease the growing tension in his muscles but it only got worse as Alex suddenly bent over to drop the apple core into the waste bin under the sink.

Stephen's teeth snapped shut with an audible click as he was treated to an excellent view of her *derrière*, temptingly encased in well-washed denim. Until that moment he'd believed himself to be well balanced about such things, preferring to take an overall view of a woman's attractions. But those tautly rounded cheeks could very well change his mind. Lord, but Alex had the loveliest rear he had ever seen!

She must have heard the sound he'd made because she glanced round and froze. There was a moment when it seemed as though both of them were caught in a spell, Alex bending over the bin, he casting undoubtedly lustful glances at her. She straightened abruptly and he was fascinated to see the wash of colour that swept up her neck, and even more fascinated to realise that it had been his scrutiny that had caused it. So she wasn't totally immune to him, then. It was the smallest of sops to his bruised ego.

'I expect you want to use the kitchen.' Her voice was more husky than chilly, although he sensed that she was trying her best to freeze it. 'I'll be out of your way just as soon as I've made myself some coffee.'

'There's no rush. I can wait till you've finished,' he replied smoothly, trying hard not to gloat. His stomach chose that moment to give an extra loud rumble and he hurried on. So much for the cool sophisticated act! 'Don't let me stop you if you're wanting to cook yourself a meal.'

'I'm not. I don't—cook, I mean.' She still sounded flustered as she started towards the door. Stephen frowned, so intrigued by what she'd said that it never crossed his mind to get out of her way.

'Then what do you do for meals?' he asked, puzzlement deepening his voice so that it seemed to grate in the silence that had fallen. He saw Alex shrug as she came to a halt when she realised he wasn't going to move out of her way. There was a flush along her elegant cheek-bones still but she returned his gaze steadily enough as she answered in a flat little monotone.

'Make myself a sandwich, have a piece of cheese and some fruit, whatever.'

'You aren't serious? Really?' He couldn't hide his astonishment. He let his gaze sweep from the top of her glorious red hair to the tips of her feet as he searched for tell-tale signs of such a deplorable diet, but there weren't any. Inch after delectable inch was perfect to his mind, although he would need to examine it closer to be absolutely certain…

His gaze soared upwards before it got him into trouble, and he saw her blush. For a nerve-racking moment he wondered if she had read his mind, and went hot and cold at the thought.

It was a relief when she rushed into speech and he realised that it was annoyance that had heightened her colour, nothing else. Lowering her defences in any way, that was obviously something she preferred not to do...at least not around him.

'*Really*. And it isn't a problem,' she stated firmly. 'I'm fit and healthy, and I'm hardly wasting away.'

'Not from the look of you,' he replied blandly, determined not to let her see how that last thought had stung. What did she have against him? he wondered for the umpteenth time, but he still had no idea of the answer.

He pushed the thought to the back of his mind, realising that he had to do something to salvage the situation before it became unbearable. After all, they were going to have to work together so they should try to get along. Maybe it would help if he tried to get to know her better, and surely this was the perfect opportunity when she had given him an opening of sorts.

Stephen gave the lightest of shrugs, disguising his interest beneath a show of indifference because he sensed it was best. 'It just seems odd, that's all. Most people cook, even if their repertoire is limited to an omelette or something simple like that.'

'I never learned how.' The words came out of their own volition so that Stephen had the impression that she immediately regretted them. He took a moment to think what to say, knowing instinctively that one wrong word would make her clam up.

'Why not? Lack of time or lack of interest?' he asked easily, moving past her to go to the old-fashioned fridge. Opening the door, he peered inside and grinned ruefully. Graham must have stocked up especially for his stay because the shelves were packed with his favourite foods, although most of it he hadn't tasted in years. Like half the population, his diet had been affected by the latest health fads so that smoked bacon, large brown eggs and whole-fat cheese hadn't even seen the inside of the fridge back at his flat!

Confining all thoughts of cholesterol to the dimmest recesses of his mind, he took out the bacon and a handful of eggs then went in search of the frying-pan, promising himself that he would get up early the next day and do an extra couple of miles jogging as a penance. Alex was still standing by the door and he wasn't sure whether she was going to answer his question or not, but he decided to give her the time and the space to make up her mind.

He carried on with what he was doing—lighting the stove, adding oil to the pan—while mentally crossing his fingers. Crazy though it sounded after their rocky start, he really did want to find out what made her tick.

'It was lack of opportunity, if you really want to know.' The admission was grudging but he didn't appreciate it any the less for that. Laying several rashers of bacon in the pan, Stephen raised an inquisitive brow.

'How come? Most girls learn to cook from their mothers, or so I've been led to believe. Wasn't your mother keen on cooking?'

'How very chauvinistic! Your true colours are really showing, Dr Spencer!' she mocked, but he didn't take offence because he sensed it was merely a ploy to delay answering the question.

'Hmm, maybe. But I'm right, aren't I? Most girls...' He gave her a wry smile as he corrected himself. 'Most *children* learn how to fend for themselves from their parents, their mothers in particular. So how come you didn't?'

She shrugged but her sea-green eyes were shadowed all of a sudden. 'Because I hardly ever saw her, or my father for that matter. They were both too busy with their careers to bother with me. My father was a top barrister before his retirement and my mother was a concert pianist.

'They employed other people to take care of me...a nanny

to teach me good manners, a maid to dress me, a chauffeur to ferry me to piano and ballet lessons and pony club meetings. And a cook to make sure that the food I ate was the very finest. The trouble was that I was never allowed anywhere near the kitchen in case I got in the way.'

She gave him an oddly tentative smile which only served to make her look even more beautiful because it lent her a sudden vulnerability. 'It came as a shock when I discovered that food didn't come all ready prepared in china dishes!'

Stephen laughed, as he'd been meant to, but that didn't mean the story hadn't affected him. Although she had glossed over the details, he sensed what a lonely childhood it had been. How ironic that they should have that in common despite the vast differences in the way they had been brought up. Alex's loneliness had stemmed from privilege, his from poverty. It was the strangest of bonds but it was a starting point, although he didn't pause to wonder why it should be so important that he found some sort of common ground they could work from.

'I see. Then it's way past time your education was completed, Dr Campbell. There should be a basin in the cupboard under the sink—get it out and beat these eggs up in it. We'll have them scrambled.'

He didn't wait to see if she would do as he said, turning away to get more bacon out of the fridge and pop it in the pan, along with the strips already sizzling away. He was conscious of a total lack of movement from her direction but he kept his attention fixed on what he was doing.

He could have cheered when she suddenly crossed the room and took the basin out of the cupboard because it felt like a small victory, not for him but for her, a way to hit back at missing out on so much of her childhood. Odd that he should feel such regret about that when he knew in his heart that she wouldn't appreciate it.

The cracking of eggshells, accompanied by the softest of curses, competed with the sizzling and he glanced round, smiling as he watched her scooping bits of eggshell out of the runny yolks. She had her lower lip caught between her teeth and her concentration was so total that she might have been performing the most delicate surgery.

She suddenly looked up and Stephen held his breath. She was as skittish as a wild bird and it would have taken very little to send her flying for cover…

'I hope you like crunchy bits in your eggs!' Her laughter came out in a sudden gust, a bit self-conscious but laughter all the same. Stephen found himself grinning back while a feeling of warmth crept into his heart. He could put up with an awful lot just to see her laugh like that more often!

'Love 'em! Now beat them to within an inch of their lives, Dr Campbell. Make sure you give them what for. Crunchy bits I can put up with but certainly not those horrible chewy white lumps you get if they're not beaten properly!'

'Yes, sir!' she retorted pertly, shooting him a mocking salute with a dripping fork. Stephen laughed as he turned his attention to the frying-pan once more while the sound of a fork being inexpertly banged around inside the basin filled the kitchen. It was like music to his ears, although he had no idea why it should be playing his tune.

'That was delicious! Especially the bacon…' Alex rolled her eyes lasciviously and Stephen laughed.

'I'd say the eggs were the best bit. I must remember to add a handful of shell to them next time…'

He ducked to avoid the screwed-up piece of kitchen roll Alex lobbed at him. He was still grinning as he got up to plug in the kettle. An hour ago the thought of Alex throwing a paper towel at him would have been about as likely as him walking on the moon. Maybe it was only a small step forward but it certainly felt like a giant leap to him!

He took cups out of the cupboard, a bit uncomfortable with that thought. Was he sure that he only wanted to improve their working relationship? Or did he really want to improve her view of him? He wasn't one hundred per cent certain which it was and it bothered him that it should matter what she thought. It was a relief when she spoke and offered a distraction from such disquieting thoughts.

'You seem to remember where everything is without any difficulty.'

'I lived here long enough, so I should do.' He grimaced as he took teabags from the old tin caddie and dropped them into the big brown pot. 'If I know Graham he won't have changed a thing. Everything will still be in the exact place it always has been.'

'I expect you're right.' She traced the grain in the top of the table with an unvarnished fingernail, a frown puckering her brow. 'How come you lived here for all that time, anyway? Are you related to Graham in some way? He's spoken about you umpteen times but he's never mentioned that you were a relative.'

'No, we aren't related. Graham just happened to be the good Samaritan who came along when I needed help, and that's how we met.' Stephen stared down at the teapot, watching as the teabags soaked up the dregs of water left in the bottom of it.

Suddenly, he wasn't sure if it was a good idea to tell her anything more. Did he really want to pour out his heart to her at this stage when it could only affect how she saw him? A shared meal and a bit of chit-chat didn't make a friendship— or much else, for that matter!

'That all sounds very mysterious—' She broke off as the phone rang, quickly pushing her chair back from the table as she got up. 'I'll get that.'

She hurried off to answer it and Stephen breathed a sigh of relief. Talk about being saved by the bell! It wasn't that he was ashamed of his past, but he wasn't proud of it either. It had always seemed more sensible to put it behind him and get on with his life. He was no longer the same person he had been—in fact, sometimes he looked back on those days with a sense of unreality, as though he were looking at something a stranger had done.

Maybe it would be better not to rush into telling Alex Campbell too much when there was little chance that she would understand. From what he had gleaned about her own background, it was a world away from his own!

He had the tea made by the time she came back, but she didn't sit down. 'I have to go out. There's a woman sick in Eden House and it sounds pretty urgent.' She glanced down at her clothes and grimaced. 'Damn! I'll have to get changed. I'd forgotten that Graham—' She stopped abruptly but Stephen knew immediately what she'd been going to say.

He put the pot on the table and smiled thinly at her. 'Forgotten that Graham wouldn't be here to take any calls tonight?'

His smile got even tighter as he saw from her expression that he'd been right. Oh, he'd realised what a poor opinion she had of him right from the moment they'd met, but he hadn't appreciated that his *professional* ability was in question as well as everything else! It was surprising how much that thought stung.

'Obviously, you've also forgotten that I'm covering for him,' he said in a deceptively mild tone, watching the tide of colour that swept up her face so betrayingly. He gave a derisive laugh, smarting from the insult she had paid him. To hell with what she thought about him *personally*, but he'd be damned if he allowed her to question his professional expertise!

'It's my turn to take any calls that come in tonight, Dr Campbell, not yours. So, please, give me the address and whatever information you have there.'

He held out his hand but Alex made no attempt to hand over the slip of paper. 'There's no need, really. I don't mind at all. I'll just go and get changed...'

She backed towards the door but Stephen stopped her by the simple expedient of catching hold of her arm. He felt the shiver that shot from his fingers hit the soles of his feet at the exact moment as he let her go, but that didn't stop the tingling from spreading to a few other areas best left unmentioned.

It was such an inappropriate response, in view of the circumstances, that his tone was harsher than ever. 'I think we need to get a few points clear from the outset. And number one on the list is that I intend to do my fair share of the work around here. I'm covering for Graham for the next six weeks, which means that I shall handle any calls that come in on his designated nights. It's the reason I opted to stay here in the house, so that I could be on hand twenty-four hours a day. So, now that we have that straight, are we going to stand here, wasting more time, while we debate this further? Or are you going to hand over those details?'

He rarely used that tone with anyone and he could tell at once that she resented it. She handed him the piece of paper in a chilly silence that spoke volumes, waiting while he read through what she had written before uttering the first frosty word.

'The family is Indian and the older members don't speak much English. One of the daughters is fluent, though, and I usually use her to interpret for me.'

'I see. And there will be no problem about me being allowed to examine this woman?' He saw the flicker of surprise in her eyes that he should be aware of the cultural difficulties often faced by a male doctor examining a female patient. However, her voice was just as frosty, making it clear that if he'd hoped to score any brownie points he had failed. Obviously, Alex Campbell was determined not to make any concessions where he was concerned!

'So long as there is a female member of the family present there shouldn't be a problem. I suggest you get Darla, the youngest daughter, to stay with you. You'll find it easier. I take it you know how to get there?' she added as an afterthought.

'Along the high street and first turning on the left.' Stephen didn't bother waiting for confirmation because he didn't need it. He knew the area like the back of his hand. It took only a few minutes to collect his jacket from upstairs.

It was still raining when he left the house, a fine drizzle which beaded on his head and shoulders as he unlocked the car door. He glanced back at the lighted kitchen window as he recalled the brief amnesty he and Alex had shared. How long had it lasted—ten minutes, fifteen, thirty at the most?

He sighed as he got into the car and started the engine. It had been nice while it had lasted but the next time they met he'd bet a pound to a penny that she would have her defences well and truly shored up again! Still, if that was the way she wanted to behave it was up to her. He certainly didn't intend to spend the next six weeks trying to win her over!

'Can you ask your mother how long she has been in pain?'

Stephen waited patiently while the teenager translated the question. He had been shown straight into the bedroom when he'd arrived and had found Mrs Bashir in bed. It was obvious that she was in a great deal of pain but the difficulty of communicating directly with her slowed things down.

He glanced around the room as Darla spoke quietly to her mother, thinking how cramped it was. Apart from the double bed in which Mrs Bashir was lying, there was also a single divan and a cot, where a plump-cheeked baby was sleeping peacefully, oblivious to what was going on.

Stephen frowned as he found himself wondering how many people were living in the flat. He'd caught a glimpse of an elderly man and woman when he'd come in, and another younger couple as well. Then there was Darla and Mrs Bashir's husband, not to mention any other children in the family. It seemed a lot of people to be crammed into such a small amount of space...

'My mother says that the pains started this morning and have got worse all day. She thought that they would stop, which is why she never called you earlier,' Darla explained as she turned to him.

Stephen nodded as he turned his attention back to his patient. 'I see. And has she any other symptoms apart from the pains in her stomach?'

Once again there was a short delay while the question was translated. Darla's liquid dark eyes skittered away from his in embarrassment. 'There is some soreness…down below… And she has had a…a discharge for a few days.'

She didn't say anything more, stepping aside while Stephen drew back the covers. 'Explain to your mother that I need to examine her tummy, will you? And I also need to know the date of her last period.'

He gently palpated the woman's abdomen, hearing the sharply indrawn breath she took. Her skin was unusually hot to the touch, making him wonder if she was running a fever. Taking a thermometer out of his case, he slipped it under her arm while he carried on with his examination, drawing back the folds of her gown to examine her legs and feet.

'Mother says that it was the end of March, maybe the twentieth.'

'But it's June now. That was three months ago.' He glanced sharply at the patient, rapidly adding up everything he'd been told. 'She isn't pregnant, I'm sure of that. Ask her if she has had a miscarriage recently, will you?'

Darla looked startled but did as she was told. Her expression was answer enough as she turned to him once more. 'Mother says that she lost the baby a week ago. I had no idea… She never told us!'

'And I don't imagine that she saw a doctor either after it happened.' Stephen checked the reading on the thermometer and sighed as he saw that it was 38°C. 'From the look of it, your mother may be suffering from puerperal sepsis. It's a bacterial infection caused by placental tissue being retained inside the body after childbirth or, in this case, miscarriage. It can be very serious as it often leads to a number of complications.'

The words were barely out of his mouth when he noticed what looked like a rash on Mrs Bashir's legs and feet. He bent down to take a closer look but it was difficult to see clearly when the only light came from a low-wattage lamp on the far side of the room.

'Can you switch the overhead light on for me, please?' he instructed, waiting while the girl hurried to do as he asked. With the benefit of better lighting, it was immediately apparent that there was indeed a rash on the woman's legs.

Stephen quickly examined the purplish blotches which extended down Mrs Bashir's legs and onto the soles of both her feet, feeling more and more concerned by what he saw. The baby had woken up with the light being switched on and now he began to grizzle softly.

Darla lifted him out of the cot, looking anxious as she saw what Stephen was looking at. 'What is it? Why has my mother got that rash?'

Stephen went to his case and took out a vial of antibiotics and a hypodermic syringe, working swiftly as he drew up the required dose. 'I'm going to give your mother an injection of antibiotics immediately. Can you explain that to her?' he instructed tersely, ignoring the question for the moment. He helped Mrs Bashir roll onto her side then swiftly gave her the injection.

Darla was watching him with terrified eyes as she rocked the baby in her arms. Stephen quickly explained what was wrong as he disposed of the used syringe.

'I think your mother may be suffering from septicaemia— blood poisoning,' he added, to make it easier for the girl to understand. 'Bacteria from the infection has passed into her bloodstream where it is rapidly multiplying. The rash is caused by the toxins.'

'And…and is it very serious?' Darla asked, her lower lip quivering as she looked at her mother.

'I'm afraid so. Your mother will need to be taken to hospital immediately. Have you a phone I can use to ring for an ambulance?'

Darla shook her head as tears slid down her cheeks. 'No, we don't have a phone of our own. We use the box at the corner of the street…'

She broke off as sobs racked her. Stephen went over and patted her arm. 'It will be all right, sweetheart. Your mother will be fine, I promise. Even now that injection of antibiotic will be starting to destroy the bacteria.'

He gave the teenager an approving smile as she wiped her eyes with the back of her hand. 'Good girl! Now, I want you to go and explain to the rest of your family what's happening. Then can you get a few things together that your mother will need—nightdress, slippers, toiletries, that sort of thing? I'll go down to my car and phone for the ambulance from there, but I'll come straight back and stay here until it arrives. All right?'

'Yes…thank you.' Darla hurried off to tell the rest of her family what was happening, while Stephen went down to make the call. One of the lifts was out of order so he took the stairs rather than wait for the other to arrive. The flat was on the eighth floor of a tower block and he mentally crossed his fingers that the other lift wouldn't break down as well. Getting Mrs Bashir down all these stairs by stretcher—that would be no mean feat!

It was well over an hour later when Stephen arrived back at the house. He drew up outside then sat for a moment, thinking back over what had happened. Mrs Bashir's husband had accompanied her in the ambulance while Darla and her older sister had followed by car. It had been obvious that the poor man had been worried sick but he had taken the time to thank Stephen in halting English for his help. It would be some time before they knew whether Mrs Bashir was out of danger but Stephen was hopeful that his swift actions had paid off.

He got out of the car and stretched luxuriously, feeling a deep sense of satisfaction at the thought. His own patients understood the value of preventative medicine and much of his time was devoted to performing health checks and giving advice.

It had been a long time since he'd felt as though he had made a real difference to anyone's life. Odd, when the reason he'd gone into medicine had been to do just that. Yet somewhere along the way he seemed to have lost sight of that aspect of the job.

He frowned as he lifted his case out of the car. When exactly had his objectives changed? He had no idea but it was rather a revelation to realise they had. It would have been nice to have talked it over with someone so that he could have got things clear in his head, but who could he talk to about something so personal? Alex Campbell? He couldn't imagine *her* being interested in his problems!

Stephen snorted in disgust at even allowing such a thought to surface as he let himself into the house. It was gone eleven and the place was in darkness apart from the hall light, which had been left burning. Obviously, Alex had gone to bed and for a moment he debated whether to stay downstairs to watch television, before deciding that he couldn't be bothered. One way or another it had been a long day—maybe bed was the best place to be.

He took a quick shower then slipped between the crisp cotton sheets with a sigh of relief. He hadn't realised until that moment just how tired he was. It had taken a lot of juggling to clear things up at his end so that he could be away for the next few weeks. Miles, his partner, hadn't been too happy about the arrangements but he'd had little choice but to go along with what Stephen had wanted...

His eyes shot open as he heard footsteps on the landing as

someone passed his door... Correction, not someone but Alex. There were only the two of them in the house so who else could it be?

The thought was decidedly unsettling, although he had no idea why it should be. Rolling onto his side, he punched the pillow into shape and closed his eyes, determined to put all thoughts of the wretched woman and her prejudices out of his mind for a few hours at least. However, the sound of water running in the bathroom next door soon had them flying open again.

Stephen lay in the darkness, listening to the sound of the bath filling. For some reason his hearing seemed to be unusually acute so that the tiniest noise sounded extra loud. He heard the squeak as the taps were turned off then a gentle splash as Alex stepped into the water. Her sigh of pleasure, however, sounded so loud to his overly sensitive ears that it was hard to believe there was a brick wall separating them. It certainly didn't prove to be any barrier to his imagination!

Stephen took a deep breath as he struggled to get a grip on himself, but it was hopeless. No matter how hard he tried to stop it, his mind carried on conjuring up a series of pictures he would have preferred not to have seen: Alex lying back in the scented water, her red hair drifting on the bubbles; Alex lifting one slender leg out of the water to soap it before letting the sponge slide up her body...

Stephen bit back a groan of dismay. He was acting like some sort of...of seedy voyeur, no matter that the pictures he was seeing weren't real but imaginary! He could just imagine Alex's reaction if she discovered that he was lying in bed, letting his mind run riot with such erotic fantasies! It would probably confirm her worst suspicions about him.

He rolled onto his stomach, pulling the blanket over his head so that he couldn't hear anything else. One day down and another forty-one to go. How on earth was he going to survive them?

CHAPTER THREE

IT WAS still raining when Stephen set out for his run the next morning. He grimaced as raindrops slithered down his neck as he jogged down the drive. For two pins he'd have turned round and gone back, only there was a doubly good reason why he should do penance.

Apart from last night's calorie-laden supper there was the small matter of how he had lain, tossing and turning most of the night, plagued by dreams he'd had absolutely no right to indulge in. Frankly, he hadn't had such X-rated dreams in years, and that they should have been triggered by Alex Campbell of all people was something that worried him. The wretched woman didn't even like him! But that small fact hadn't made a scrap of difference as his mind had run riot.

Stephen's mouth compressed as he picked up speed, using the exercise to put all thought of the ill-fated night out his head. It was only a little after six and there were few people about at that time of the morning so he was able to slip into an easy loping stride, without the danger of running anyone down.

He turned left when he reached the end of the road, his powerful legs eating up the pavement so that in no time at all he came to the park. The gates were never locked so he turned in through them and began a circuit of the path bordering the balding grass, grimacing as he noticed how unkempt the whole place looked.

Council cut-backs were obviously in force so that the flower-beds he recalled from his childhood were no more than a distant memory. It grieved him that the people in the area didn't have even this small patch of green to come to to escape the dreary concrete tower blocks where they lived.

He couldn't imagine the residents of his neighbourhood putting up with such a lack of amenities but, then, they had the money and its consequent influence to make their views known. It was rather a sobering thought.

Three circuits of the park later, Stephen was beginning to puff. He slowed down, using the sweatband around his wrist to wipe the perspiration from his eyes. The rain had stopped at last but the sky was still grey. A movement off to his right caught his attention, and he frowned as he saw a boy of about eight or nine, kicking a football about. It was barely seven even now, early for a child to be out on his own, playing.

The football suddenly shot across the path in front of him, almost tripping him up. Stephen came to a halt and bent down to retrieve it as the boy came running over to him.

'Sorry, mister.' The child held out his hands for the ball and Stephen tossed it to him with a grin.

'That's OK. No damage done. What are you doing here by yourself, anyway? It's a bit early to be out playing, isn't it?'

The boy shrugged as he scuffed the toe of his worn trainers along a crack in the tarmac. 'I was fed up being in on me own.'

Stephen frowned. 'On your own? Where are your parents, then? Have they gone to work?'

The child looked suddenly wary as he began edging away. 'Mum'll be back soon. I have to go…' He stopped abruptly as he caught sight of something. Stephen turned to see what it was and saw a young woman hurrying towards them. It wasn't hard to spot the resemblance between her and the child because they shared the same delicate features and fine blond hair, although he wasn't sure what relation she was to the boy. His sister possibly? She certainly didn't look old enough to be his mother.

'What are you doing here, Danny? Haven't I told you that you are *never* to go out on your own like this?'

Anxiety contorted her face as she slid her arm protectively

around the boy's shoulders, before turning to look uneasily at Stephen. He quickly set about introducing himself, realising how worried she must be to find a stranger talking to the child.

'Hello, there, I'm Stephen Spencer. I'm standing in for Dr Barker for the next six weeks.' He gave young Danny a quick smile. 'He must be a keen footballer if he's eager to get out at this time of the morning to practise!'

The young woman looked a little happier once she knew who he was. 'He shouldn't be out here on his own. Anything could have happened to him and nobody would have known. Usually my neighbour, Mrs Bashir, listens out for him while I'm at work, but she was rushed into hospital last night.'

That explained things. Stephen nodded understandingly. 'Oh, I see. Unfortunately, Mrs Bashir was extremely ill so I doubt whether she or her family had a chance to think about Danny.'

'Oh, I realised that as soon as I heard what had happened. Neelam…Mrs Bashir…would never have left Danny on his own if she could have avoided it. She's been wonderful, a real friend. I don't know how I would have managed without her…' The young woman flushed in embarrassment. 'I'm sorry. You don't want to waste your time, listening to my problems, Dr…'

'Spencer,' Stephen repeated when she hesitated. He gave her a warm smile, noticing how strained she looked. There were dark circles under her eyes and a pinched look to her mouth which told of too little sleep and too much worry. 'And you aren't wasting my time at all. It's nice to meet you and Danny. I'm only here for a few weeks so it's good to break the ice, so to speak, in case you ever need to see me in a professional capacity, although I'm certainly not touting for business!'

The young woman laughed at that. 'I'm sure you're not. From what I've seen of the surgery, your days will be full enough, without drumming up trade!' She sighed as she shot a glance at the boy, who had edged away and was kicking the ball about once more. 'I've made more than my fair share of visits to Dr Barker over the past eight years, I'm afraid. He's been marvellous, the way he's looked after Danny. Nothing is ever too much trouble for him.'

'Dr Barker is certainly a wonderful doctor,' Stephen agreed immediately. He frowned as he shot an enquiring glance at the child. 'What's been wrong with Danny? He looks very fit to me.'

'He's got haemophilia,' she answered sadly. 'He's fine at the moment, thank heavens, but things can go wrong so quickly. He's mad on football but this is the only time he ever gets to play—by himself and when there's nobody else about. He'd give anything to be able to come to the park and play with his friends but I've warned him that he must never do that.'

'It must be very hard for him,' Stephen sympathised, his heart going out to the boy. Being banned from playing any contact sports must be hard for the child but necessary, given his condition. Stephen had treated several haemophiliacs over the years, but all had been adults who had understood the dangers inherent to the dangerous bleeding disorder.

A deficiency of the blood protein, Factor VIII, meant that their blood-clotting mechanism was defective and bleeding could occur either spontaneously or as the result of an injury. Allowing Danny to take part in any kind of sport where he could be injured, that was too big a risk to take.

'It is—hard for him, I mean.' The young woman sighed. 'It's all my fault, too. They explained that at the hospital the first time I took Danny there, when Dr Barker realised there was a real problem. They told me that it's all because of a defective gene and that I passed it on to him.'

Well, that explained the relationship between the pair. Obviously she was Danny's mother, although Stephen still found it hard to believe as she looked little more than a child herself. However, he was less concerned with that than the fact that she sounded so guilty. He quickly set about making her understand that she wasn't to blame herself for something she had no control over.

'You're right that the defective gene is passed through the mother but, unless there is reason to suspect there might be a problem, few women realise they are carriers of it. I take it that there was no history of haemophilia in your family?'

She gave him a tight smile. 'I wouldn't know. I was brought up in care, you see. So I had no contact with my family.'

She turned away, leaving Stephen feeling as though he had put his foot in it. Waving to Danny, who came running over to join them, she turned back to Stephen, and he was glad to see that she didn't appear to be upset about his unwitting gaffe. 'Well, we'd better get back home or Danny will be late for school. It was nice meeting you, Dr Spencer.'

'And you, too.' Stephen gave the pair a wide smile. 'Don't take this the wrong way, but let's hope I don't see you again too soon, or at least not in the surgery!'

They all laughed at the quip before they parted company. Stephen jogged to the gate and paused to glance back, watching as Danny and his mother hurried across the field towards the gate at the far side of the park. It led out into the road where Eden House was situated; he could see the block of flats towering above the surrounding streets.

There were two more blocks of flats as well, Adam House and Eve House, both of them twenty-odd stories high, faceless grey blocks of concrete which housed hundreds of people.

He sighed as he started back to the surgery. They were no place to bring up a child. Whoever had decided to stack families one on top of the other like that should be shot!

The sun was just starting to peep through the clouds by the time Stephen arrived back at the surgery. He let himself in and went straight to the kitchen to get a drink, before going upstairs to shower. He elbowed the door open, busily dragging the sweat-stained T-shirt over his head as he did so. Stopping to talk to Danny and his mother had delayed him and he was conscious that time was ticking away. He most certainly didn't want to be late and give Alex anything else to gripe about!

That thought had barely crossed his mind when he became aware of music issuing from the room. With the T-shirt half on and half off he was somewhat hampered from seeing what was going on. He dragged the shirt the rest of the way over his head then came to a halt as he found himself face to face with Alex. She was sitting at the kitchen table, a glass of orange juice poised halfway to her lips as though she had stopped dead in the middle of drinking it.

Stephen felt his heart give a sudden lurch as he saw the expression on her face, a mixture of surprise and something which he was chary about putting a name to. Interest? Awareness? Appreciation even? He wasn't sure which but it was fascinating to wonder if it was the sight of him which had prompted it!

'Sorry. I didn't realise you were in here,' he said quickly, before his ego got him into trouble. He draped the T-shirt around his neck, suddenly self-conscious about the amount of his bare flesh on view. He knew he was in good shape, the jogging and other exercise he took on a regular basis having whittled away any spare ounces of fat which might otherwise have clung to his large frame. However, that didn't mean that Alex appreciated the sight over her breakfast...

Oh, no! his ego jeered, refusing to give up that easily. If she didn't like what she saw, why was she staring?

Stephen swung round and strode to the fridge to pour himself some orange juice, afraid that his face would give him away. OK, so she *was* staring and she *didn't* look shocked, but so what? He was aiming to work with the wretched woman, not seduce her!

Alex switched off the radio and stood up, smiling thinly as Stephen glanced round. 'You are aware that we start surgery at eight sharp each morning, Dr Spencer? Graham did mention it?

Her tone was, well—waspish was the best adjective he could come up with. It certainly stung Stephen into marshalling his thoughts. 'Yes, he mentioned it, thank you, Dr Campbell.'

Her green eyes glinted as he mocked her formality by using her full title. She drew herself up, her beautiful face looking as though it had been carved from the purest marble, so cold and expressionless was it. 'He must not have mentioned, however, that we try to have a brief discussion beforehand about any problems we've encountered the previous day. Both morning and evening surgeries are always so busy that it's impossible to fit it in any other time, especially when there are house calls to attend to as well.'

'It sounds like an excellent idea to me. Two heads are often better than one—isn't that right, Dr Campbell?' He kept his tone just as impersonal, not allowing even a hint of emotion to warm it. His smile was just as detached as he treated Alex to it. Two could play at this game, he decided. If she persisted in acting this way he'd be damned if he'd try to break down the barriers again.

'Exactly.' She gave him a tight smile in return, her face betraying as little as his did, and yet for some reason Stephen sensed that she was hurt. Why? Because he'd treated her to a dose of her own medicine? Ridiculous! Yet as she left the room he couldn't shake off the feeling.

Stephen sighed as he plugged in the kettle and made himself a cup of coffee to take upstairs. Why should it matter if she was hurt by his response? She was a grown woman and she should be prepared to take what she dished out. But he knew in his heart that it bothered him. And *that* worried him more than anything else. He was far too sensitive to Alex Campbell's feelings...whatever they were!

Stephen was seated behind the desk in Graham's consulting room when the old clock in the hall struck the quarter-hour. He looked up as Alex tapped on the open door.

'Come in,' he said easily, rising from his seat to wave her towards the chair in front of the desk. He waited until she'd sat down, before taking his seat again. 'I wasn't sure what the routine was so I thought it would be easier to come straight in here and wait till you found me.'

'That's fine,' she replied shortly, carefully smoothing her plain grey skirt over her knees. She was wearing a crisp white blouse with it, the cuffs neatly buttoned at each wrist, and low-heeled black leather shoes. Her hair was once again coiled at the nape of her neck, her face devoid of make-up, apart from a trace of lip gloss which somehow only served to highlight the ripeness of her mouth.

Stephen found his gaze drawn to the sensuous fullness of her lips before he deliberately averted his gaze. He and Alex Campbell were colleagues, nothing more. How she looked or what she wore didn't enter into the equation. If he repeated it often enough surely it would sink in?

'There was just one case I'd appreciate hearing your views on, Dr Spencer.'

The formal note in her voice brought his thoughts squarely back on track. 'I'd be glad to help in any way I can. What's the problem?' he offered immediately.

Alex frowned as she picked up the file of notes she'd brought with her and handed it to him. 'The patient is a teenage girl called Letitia Churchill. I've seen her a couple of times in the past month but I can't seem to get to the bottom of what's wrong with her.'

'I see.' Stephen quickly read through the notes, surprised to find how few there were. 'What's happened to the rest of her file? Has she recently transferred to this practice and we're waiting for the rest of her notes to arrive, or what?'

'Letitia was living in Jamaica until six months ago. She was born in England but her parents moved back there when she was ten. She's come back to England to live with her aunt while she continues her education.'

Alex picked up a pen from the desk and began to doodle on a scrap of paper, making him wonder if she was nervous before he realised how unlikely that was. What did she have to be nervous about? Him? No way!

'And you've taken that into consideration, I imagine?' His tone was curt as he struggled not to let her know that his mind had been wandering.

'You mean the fact that her illness might be related to where she lived previously?' she queried just as tersely. She suddenly sighed as she dropped the pen onto the desk. 'Yes, I have. The trouble is that I don't have any real hands-on experience of tropical medicine. All I know is what I've read about in text-books and it doesn't seem to be much help in this case. What do you think, Stephen? Is there anything you can think of which I may have missed?'

He couldn't deny the pleasure he felt at hearing her call him by his given name at last. However, he was wary about letting her see how it affected him because he sensed that she would immediately retreat into her icy shell.

'I'll certainly try to come up with something if I can,' he replied levelly, focusing firmly on the problem in front of him. 'I've always been interested in tropical medicine, funnily enough. I studied at Liverpool, which has one of the finest schools of tropical medicine in the country. I think that was what whetted my interest. So, for starters, let's see what symptoms we have.'

Alex didn't say anything as he read through the brief notes more thoroughly. It was an interesting case and he was soon engrossed. He frowned thoughtfully as he recited the symptoms out loud. 'Loss of appetite and consequential weight loss, inflammation of the mouth and tongue... Any signs of anaemia?'

He glanced up, frowning even harder when Alex nodded. 'Yes. I ordered a blood test and the results came back yesterday.' She handed him the slip of paper from the laboratory. 'As you can see, they show megaloblastic anaemia.'

'Hmm, interesting. That type of anaemia is caused by a deficiency of vitamin B12 and/or folic acid,' Stephen replied thoughtfully. 'You checked that the patient has a balanced diet, I imagine?'

'Yes. That was the first thing I thought of, given her age. However, Letitia and her aunt both assured me that she hasn't been dieting, nor is she vegan—that can cause this sort of problem in many cases. She regularly eats meat, fish and dairy products, all the main sources of vitamin B12, plus a lot of green vegetables, which should have maintained her folic acid level. Apparently, she has a good appetite normally, although recently she hasn't wanted to eat very much at all,' Alex replied immediately.

'Good.' Stephen smiled at her. 'It's always best to check the basics first. It's only too easy to overlook them in the search for something more exciting to blame for a patient's illness!'

She laughed softly. 'You sound just like Graham. That's one of the things he always stresses—look for the most obvious cause first before you start digging through the textbooks!'

Stephen laughed as well, his face softening at the comparison. 'Well, I'll take that as a compliment. Graham is one of the finest doctors I've ever met. It's good to know that we're on the same wavelength, although it's not that surprising. It's only natural that some of his ideas should have rubbed off.'

He turned back to the notes again, suddenly realising that he was in danger of saying more than he should. Once again the thought that Alex might find much about his past not to her liking surfaced, along with the niggling little question of why it should matter what she thought.

'I see that you've prescribed vitamin B12 tablets and a folic acid supplement?' he queried, pushing the unsettling thought to the back of his mind as he read through the previous day's report.

'Yes, although I'm not happy about simply treating the symptoms. It really isn't enough, is it?' She leaned forward and her expression was earnest all of a sudden. 'I need to find out what's really wrong with Letitia then see what can be done about it!'

'I agree.' Stephen nodded his approval and earned himself a tentative smile. He looked back at the notes, surprised by how pleased he felt to be on the receiving end of such a small token. He'd had women treat him to a lot more than a smile and not felt so buoyed up about it, if he were truthful, which he had no intention of being at that moment!

His finger came to rest on a note Graham had made several weeks earlier, and he looked up enquiringly. 'It says here that the patient suffered bouts of diarrhoea?'

'Yes. Letitia mentioned it almost in passing at the time. Graham said that she was very embarrassed when he tried to question her further. I asked her yesterday if she'd had any recurrence of it but she denied it.' Alex sighed as she sat back and crossed her legs so that the grey skirt slid an inch or two above her shapely knees. 'I don't think she was telling me the truth, to be honest.'

'You could be right. I've an idea what this might be, and if I'm right then diarrhoea is a recurring problem.'

Stephen got up and crossed the room to take one of the reference books off a shelf, not at all loath to remove himself from the tempting sight of those slender, nylon-clad legs, which was hardly conducive to cogent thought. Riffling through the pages, he came to what he wanted and skimmed through the text.

'I thought so...' he muttered, going back to the desk to lay the weighty tome in front of Alex so that she could read it as well. He bent down to point out the section in question and caught a waft of her perfume. He straightened abruptly and moved away to stand by the window while she read the page, wondering why he found that particular perfume such a stimulant. He couldn't recall being so affected by a scent before, yet every cell in his body seemed to be humming...

'It all seems to fit perfectly, doesn't it?'

The delight in her voice had him turning round and he felt his head spin as she treated him to a dazzling smile. It was an effort to keep his tone even when he replied and that was definitely scary. He liked women and they liked him, but he'd always been the one in charge of any relationships in the past, the one to take the initiative, whether it was starting them or ending them. Yet he knew with a sudden alarming insight that where Alex was concerned it wasn't that simple!

'It does.' He cleared his throat, praying that she would attribute the husky note it held to excitement at possibly solving the mystery. 'Tropical sprue is a disorder of the intestines not unlike coeliac disease, but in this case it isn't an intolerance to gluten that causes the problem. This disease means that the patient suffers from chronic malabsorption and has trouble absorbing any carbohydrates and minerals.'

'So that he could literally die of malnutrition even though he, or rather in this case she, is eating properly?' Alex shook her head. 'It's incredible when you think about it, isn't it? I've read about it, of course, but how did you work out what it might be so quickly?'

'I've seen it before,' he admitted, trying not to let himself get carried away by the admiration in her beautiful voice.

He frowned, wondering when he'd taken note of the fact that it *was* beautiful. At some point he must have absorbed how those husky tones were just the right pitch and volume to form such a seductive blend...

He cleared his throat once more, aware that Alex was watching him with the faintest frown beginning to pucker her brow at his continued silence.

'It was some time ago that I came across it, while I was still a student, in fact. I was doing my pre-registration at the Royal in Liverpool when there was a patient admitted, exhibiting many of the symptoms Letitia has shown. He was in a very bad state and it was touch and go whether he'd pull through.

He was from the Far East and he'd tried a lot of herbal remedies, before contacting his GP who immediately referred him to us.'

'So, what happened?' Alex frowned as she glanced back at the textbook. 'There doesn't seem to be very much here about what sort of treatment should be given, apart from vitamin and mineral supplements.' She looked up and her deep green eyes were serious as they met his. 'Surely there must be more to it than that?'

Stephen ran his hand through his immaculately groomed hair purely for want of something to do. Being treated to the full force of that glorious green gaze was deeply unsettling.

Had she any idea just how beautiful she was? he found himself wondering. She must do! And yet there was no trace of artifice in the way she looked at him, no hint of that coquettishness most beautiful women used almost unconsciously. It made it even more difficult to understand what made her tick!

'If it is tropical sprue, and we need to have that confirmed before we do anything else, then I'm afraid there is no quick and easy cure,' he explained carefully, forcing his attention back to what they were discussing.

He turned back to the window, opting for the uninspiring view of the street rather than the far more appealing one of the woman seated in front of the desk. 'Bed rest and a high-protein diet to begin with, plus treatment for the anaemia and other vitamin deficiencies. Large doses of vitamin B complex, plus A and D and calcium supplements—the full works, in fact. Because tropical sprue is thought to be the result of an intestinal infection, antibiotics are usually given and do seem to work. However, it could take some time for her to recover, I'm afraid.'

'Poor Letitia! She was telling me that she's hoping to start college this September, too.' Alex sounded upset.

Stephen glanced round, surprised to see real regret on her face. Somehow he hadn't expected that she would become so involved with a patient. She appeared so detached that it came as a shock to realise how much she cared. Maybe it was only when she was dealing with certain people that she acted so distantly—like with him, for instance. It was a salutory thought.

He went back to the desk and sat down, refusing to let himself dwell on it. 'I think we should try to be positive. At least the girl has been sensible enough to seek help so there's every chance that if it is sprue we can get it under control. I suggest you get on to the hospital and make an appointment for her to be seen by the consultant there.'

'You're right, of course. She'll need a jejunal biopsy, won't she?' she queried immediately.

'That's right. The only way to check if it is sprue is to take a sample from the small intestine. In the meantime, at least you have the comfort of knowing that you prescribed exactly the right course of treatment for Letitia so she won't get any worse.'

'Thank heavens for that!' Alex smiled narrowly when his brows rose. 'I was getting cold feet at the thought that you might tell me I'd done entirely the wrong thing.'

Stephen laughed incredulously. 'That I don't believe! I can't imagine you ever getting nervous about anything.'

'No?' She stood up abruptly, smoothing her skirt over her hips in a gesture which might have seemed flirtatious in anyone else. However, Stephen was sure that it was practicality which had prompted it, not a bid to draw his attention to the shapeliness of her hips and thighs...

He closed his mind to such unprofessional observations as he realised that she had continued speaking, and he frowned as he heard what she was saying.

'Graham told me what a perfectionist you are, Stephen. I think he was trying to warm me to be on my toes, so it's little wonder that I'm nervous, isn't it?'

'A perfectionist... Me?' He frowned even harder as he considered that idea. He glanced up when she laughed but there was little warmth in the sound and even less in the look she gave him.

'Yes, you. I suppose it explains a lot of things.' She glanced around the room, her eyes moving deliberately over the shabby furnishings before coming back to look squarely at him across the desk.

'I don't expect you could face working here full time. It must be light years away from how things are at your own practice. I suppose it's just about bearable, putting in a few weeks to help Graham out, but imagine working here on a permanent basis. It would be a nightmare for someone like you, Stephen, who's only happy with the very best.'

She gave him a last thin smile then left the room before he could say anything. Not that he could think of much to say. The sheer surprise of that challenging statement seemed to have emptied his head of everything else.

He got up abruptly and went back to the window, but he barely saw the dismal view this time. A perfectionist—was that what he was? Someone who demanded the highest standards in every aspect of his life?

Perhaps it should be taken as a compliment but Alex hadn't meant it as such. He was certain of that! Did she *really* believe that he was so shallow that he put such store on wealth and possessions and little else, because that was the impression she had given him now that he thought about it.

He turned to look around the shabby room while, unbidden, the image of his own elegantly appointed surgery sprang to mind. The two places were worlds apart, as she'd said, but which one did he fit into? He had striven so hard for everything he'd achieved to date, and a private practice in the best area of the city had to be every GP's dream. But was it what he *really* wanted? Was he completely happy?

It was as though a veil had been torn aside and he was looking at his life clearly for the first time in ages. It shocked him to realise that, despite achieving everything he'd set out to, there was something missing from his life. He'd been aware of it for some time but had tried to ignore it. Now Alex's words made that impossible any longer and he was suddenly afraid.

If he didn't want what he had then what did he want? He had no idea but deep down he knew that the coming weeks were going to change his whole life. Whether it would be for the better or for the worse he had no way of knowing, just as he had no idea what part Alex Campbell was going to play in it. Perhaps *that* was the most disturbing thought of all!

CHAPTER FOUR

THE morning flew past. Stephen was amazed by the number of patients who needed to be seen. The pace at his own practice was far more leisurely, appointments being spaced further apart to allow more time for each consultation. However, the sheer volume of people requiring attention didn't allow for that luxury here. It worried him that he might miss something so he tried not to rush, but it was hard not to feel pressurised.

When Dorothy tapped on his door between appointments with a much-needed cup of coffee he greeted her with relief. 'Am I glad to see you? Thanks.' He took a sip of the fortifying brew, shuddering appreciatively as the caffeine kicked into his system. 'Is it always this hectic around here?'

Dorothy sighed as she glanced back at the crowded waiting-room. 'Always! I can't remember the last day when we didn't run over time. Frankly, I don't know how Alex has coped recently. The poor girl has been run off her feet.'

Stephen frowned as he took another sip of coffee. 'What do you mean by that? You make it sound as though she's been shouldering the brunt of the work.'

'And so she has.' Dorothy looked round then quickly closed the door so that nobody could overhear their conversation. 'To be honest, Stephen, I've been worried sick about how things have been going around here. Dr Barker has done his best but he hasn't been well. There's been many a time when it was obvious that he shouldn't have been at work, but he kept soldiering on.'

'I see.' Stephen took a deep breath but it did little to ease the guilt he felt. He should never have allowed Graham to fob him off with assurances that he was fine. 'So I take it that more of the workload has been falling on Dr Campbell's shoulders, then? How did she feel about that? A lot of young doctors would have resented it.'

'Not her!' Dorothy stated firmly. 'Frankly, that girl has been a godsend. Not once has she ever grumbled about the amount of work she's had to do, unlike that Peter who was here before her.' The elderly receptionist sniffed.

'He spent most of his time griping about how overworked he was, but he didn't take on half the responsibility Alex has. Many a day she's had a quiet word with me and told me to send as many patients in to see her as possible if Dr Barker has looked particularly bad. This place wouldn't have kept going these past months if it hadn't been for her. Still, now that you're here, Stephen, it will take the pressure off her, won't it?'

Dorothy excused herself as the phone started ringing. Stephen frowned thoughtfully. What he'd learned was deeply disquieting and not just because it made him feel so guilty. That Alex had been run ragged, trying to keep things ticking over, *and* had done so willingly forced him to view her in a different light, and that in itself was unsettling. He'd had an inkling only that morning that she wasn't the dispassionate professional she made herself out to be and now here was more proof.

So what was she really like? He had no idea, but this new facet to her character didn't make it any easier to understand her, and that was what he would dearly like to do. Whether she would appreciate his interest, however, was open to question!

It was well after midday before Stephen came to the end of his list. The majority of cases he'd seen had been the usual mix of coughs and colds and minor infections. However, there had been a worrying number of chronic illnesses to deal with, the most notable of which was asthma.

Stephen frowned as he glanced through the relevant case notes as he made his way to the office. Three adults and one child had been to see him, all suffering from breathing problems. Maybe it was to be expected in such an area, when people daily breathed in pollutants, but it was worrying all the same…

'Dr Spencer…help me!'

Stephen swung round as he heard the frantic cry. It took him only a second to react to the scene which met his eyes. He ran down the corridor and quickly lifted Danny out of his mother's arms. 'What happened?' he demanded, leading the way into his room where he put the child down on the couch.

'I'm not sure…' The young woman took a wobbly breath as she struggled to compose herself. 'Danny always comes home for his lunch. It's safer than him staying at school and getting pushed around in the playground. I realised he was late and went down to see if I could see him and found him by the lifts. I…I think someone must have hit him!'

'From the look of him, you could be right.' Stephen's tone was grim as he gently turned the child's face towards the light so that he could examine the cut along his cheek-bone. It was bleeding profusely, as was a smaller cut on his chin. Tears were trickling down the boy's face as well, making it even more difficult to see how much damage had been done, but Stephen knew that he had to assess the extent of his injuries as quickly as possible.

'I know it hurts, Danny, but I want you to be really brave and help me out here,' he said softly, using a wad of tissues to wipe the boy's face. 'I need to know exactly where it hurts so that I can see how much damage has been done. OK?'

The soothing tone helped to quieten the sobbing child and he sniffed noisily then added. 'A' right.'

'Good boy!' Stephen patted his shoulder then went to the desk to fetch the tiny torch he used for examining eyes. 'I'm just going to shine this light into your eyes, son,' he explained, tilting Danny's chin. He shone the light into each eye in turn and was relieved to see that both pupils reacted evenly, thereby ruling out the possibility of pressure being exerted on the brain from internal bleeding.

'That's great. Now, apart from your cheek and chin, where else does it hurt?' he asked as he put the torch down.

'My hip…this one.' Danny rolled over so that Stephen could examine his left hip, wincing as Stephen gently peeled his trousers away. His hip was already heavily bruised, because of the amount of blood which was rapidly collecting in the area, and looked extremely painful.

'Right, I can see why that hurts all right. What a whopper of a bruise! It's a good job it isn't by your eye or you'd have a real shiner,' he teased, and was pleased when the child gave a half-hearted grin.

He turned to Danny's mother once again, his heart going out to her as he saw the worry on her face. Something like this must have been her worst nightmare, given the child's medical condition. Deliberately, he adopted a bracing tone.

'Well, it isn't too bad, despite how it looks. I'm going to give Danny some Factor VIII to control the bleeding. Then I'd like him to go to hospital for a brain scan, just to be on the safe side, although I'm not anticipating that they will find anything wrong. But we'll get him cleaned up a bit first. My reputation will be in tatters if people see him leaving here in this state, and on my first day in the practice, too!'

He turned away as the child's mother laughed shakily, obviously reassured by his tone, and only then realised that Alex was standing in the doorway. There was the strangest expression on her face, but before he could work out what it meant she beckoned him over.

'Dorothy told me what had happened,' she said in a low voice as he went to join her. 'I thought you might need a hand but obviously you've got things under control. I wasn't sure if you knew that Danny was a haemophiliac.'

'As luck would have it, I came across him and his mother

this morning when I was out, running, and she told me about his condition. But thanks anyway. I appreciate it.' He gave her a warm smile and was surprised to see a touch of colour run up her cheeks.

She looked away, her gaze centring on the boy, so that Stephen found it impossible to tell what she was thinking. However, her tone wasn't quite as even as usual as she continued.

'That was lucky. At least it meant that you knew straight away how serious this could be. Danny doesn't have the disease in its severest form, thankfully. But the percentage of Factor VIII in his blood does mean that he suffers the odd spontaneous bleed, and severe bleeding after minor injuries. Prompt treatment is essential.'

'I worked on that assumption,' Stephen replied levelly, pushing all thoughts of what might be wrong with Alex to the back of his mind while he concentrated on the patient. 'I take it that Graham keeps some Factor VIII in stock in case of emergencies like this? I'd like to give Danny an injection right away. Although I'm fairly confident there won't be a major problem, it needs attending to immediately.'

'Of course. I'll show you where everything is kept.'

Alex quickly led the way along the corridor to the storeroom, collecting the key on their way from a drawer in the office desk. She unlocked the door then switched on the light and went straight to the small refrigerator, where some of the drugs were stored to maintain them at their optimum temperature.

She glanced round as she opened the refrigerator door, the interior light bouncing fiery sparks off her red hair and making it glow. Stephen took a quick breath as every cell in his body responded to the sight. She was so beautiful that he would have needed to have been a monk not to have been aware of it! Yet letting her know how attracted he was to her was out of the question. It would be totally unprofessional *and* exceedingly foolish when she'd made it plain what her opinion of him was!

'Graham makes a point of always keeping freeze-dried Factor VIII on hand in case Danny needs it. He has a soft spot for the boy and for Debbie, his mother,' Alex explained, taking what they needed out of the fridge and handing it to him.

'She seems very young to have a child that age,' Stephen observed, automatically checking the instructions for reconstituting the drug.

Alex sighed as she closed the refrigerator and led the way back into the corridor. 'I believe she was just eighteen when she had Danny.' She locked the storeroom door then headed back to the office to return the key. Dorothy must have gone for her lunch while they'd been busy because there was no sign of her when Stephen glanced into the room.

Alex slipped the key back into the drawer, before continuing the tale. 'It's quite a sad story, actually. Debbie was brought up in care and never knew her own family. When she left the children's home she moved down here, attracted by the bright city lights, I imagine. Anyway, she managed to get herself a job in a solicitor's office—just clerical work, you understand, but it was a start.

'Unfortunately, she got involved with one of the partners in the practice, a man who was a lot older than she was and far more experienced.' She gave Stephen a wry look. 'You can guess the rest of the story, I expect?'

'She got pregnant and this guy didn't want to know?' His mouth thinned with sudden anger. The tale had hit a bit too close to home and it was difficult to hide his feelings. 'Oh, I can guess how it went all right. It isn't that difficult, is it? Too many men walk away scot-free in situations like that, leaving the women to carry the can!'

Alex frowned. 'That sounds as though you're speaking from personal experience?'

'I am!' He saw the start she gave at the vehemence in his tone and sighed. 'My mother found herself in much the same situation as Debbie did. She brought me up on her own and, believe me, it wasn't easy for her.'

'I'm sorry. I had no idea…' She sounded surprised. Reaching out, she laid her hand on his arm in an instinctive gesture of comfort that startled them both. There was a moment when tension hummed between them. Stephen knew that he was holding his breath. He could feel the warm imprint of her fingers through his shirtsleeves, feel that same warmth spreading along his arm until it seemed to fill his whole body, creating the strangest sensations.

Could Alex feel it too? he wondered. This deep sense of closeness which enveloped them at that moment, as though by the simple act of touching they had forged some kind of bond…

She withdrew her hand abruptly, keeping her face averted so that he had no way of knowing if she had felt it. 'I'd better not keep you any longer. Danny needs that injection. Did…did I hear you mention something about him going to hospital for a scan?'

The husky note in her voice made him want to reach out and touch her, but suddenly he knew that would be a mistake. Already she was regretting the lowering of her defences and maybe he should regret it, too, regret that urge he'd had to disclose something so personal. It was hard to understand why he had done it.

He never talked about his childhood; not even his partner, Miles, knew about his background. The memories were too personal to share with others when they might end up as a source of gossip. Yet he knew instinctively that anything he told Alex would be treated in confidence and with compassion. Funny, but realising that seemed to warm a part of his heart which had been cold for a long time.

It was an effort not to show how shaken he felt by the discovery but he tried his best to disguise it. There had been quite enough revelations for one day!

'That's right. I'd like to rule out any possibility of bleeding in the brain. Danny hasn't said what happened yet but, from the look of him, I'd say someone punched him. You can't be too careful in a situation like his, given his history.'

'How dreadful! He's such a lovely little boy, too. He never complains even though it can't be much fun for him, not being able to go out and play with his friends.' Alex's green eyes flashed with sudden fire as she glanced towards the consulting room. 'If I knew who'd done this to him...'

Stephen laughed softly and she flicked him an uncertain glance. 'What's so funny?'

'Only that when I first met you I had you summed up as the proverbial ice maiden. You were certainly frosty enough to me,' he teased.

'I treat people as I find them.' There was an unmistakable challenge in the look she gave him. 'If I feel a situation calls for a certain degree of detachment then that's how I respond to it.'

Meaning that was the treatment he warranted? Stephen longed to ask why but pride forbade it. He gave her a thin smile, not allowing any hint of curiosity to touch his grey eyes. If she was hoping that he would demand an explanation, hard luck. Whatever prejudices she had about him, she was welcome to them!

'I see. It must be a great comfort to you, Dr Campbell, to be able to compartmentalise your feelings so effectively.'

He saw that the jibe had hit home by the way her eyes flashed. Score one for me! he thought drily, before forcing himself to behave like the professional he was. 'I'd like to run Debbie and Danny to the hospital myself. Will that cause a problem? I was rostered for house calls this afternoon.'

'There's no need to worry. I'll do them.' She turned on her heel then stopped as a sudden thought struck her. 'I almost forgot. I'm due at Arden House this afternoon.'

'The old people's home at the end of the street?' Stephen

queried. He shrugged when she nodded. 'That isn't a problem. I'll take over from you. What time were you due there?'

'Between two-thirty and three. We go there once a fortnight to make routine checks on any resident who's receiving treatment and pick up on anything new which has cropped up. The majority of the residents have limited mobility so we find it easier to go to them rather than have them brought into the surgery. Dorothy should have left all the case notes ready in the tray.'

'Fine. No problem. I'll see you later, then.' Stephen watched as she hurried away. He sighed as he made his way back to Debbie and Danny. One step forward and three back seemed to be the order of the day around Alex. Maybe he should just accept that she wasn't interested in fostering a better relationship between them, but it wasn't easy. Working—and living— in such close proximity, that made it nigh on impossible to ignore her.

'Not seen you before, young man. 'Ere, Gertie, 'ow about 'im, then? Bit of an improvement on Dr Barker, lovely man though he is, ain't he? Should do wonders for me bunions, and everything else!'

The old lady gave a cackling laugh as she drew her friend's attention to Stephen's presence. He grinned, shaking his head as the matron, who was showing him round the rest home, wagged an admonishing finger.

'I don't mind, honestly,' he assured the pleasant, middle-aged woman, whose name he had learned was Meg Parker. 'She seems a lively old soul.'

'You can say that again!' Meg replied with a heartfelt sigh. 'Elsie leads us all a merry dance, don't you, love?'

'What's the point in living if you don't 'ave a bit of fun? Place like this could get you down otherwise.' The old lady patted the stool next to her chair with an age-gnarled hand. 'Come on, 'andsome. You come an' sit yourself down by me.

It's been a long time since a smashin' young fellow has come callin' on me!'

Stephen laughed as he sat down. 'I don't believe that. What's wrong with the men around here? Are they blind or something?'

Elsie laughed delightedly, showing a mouthful of teeth so perfectly even and white that they had to be false. 'Now 'ere's a man who really *does* know 'ow to treat a lady. Not like that other young fellow who used to come, Peter somethin' or other. He was real po-faced. Couldn't take a joke at all. Anyway, 'ow come you're workin' for Dr Barker?'

She leaned over and fingered the lapel of Stephen's jacket, admiring the fine wool. 'Lovely bit o' cloth that, and I should know what I'm talkin' about. My Sidney was one of the best tailors in this 'ere city and 'e taught me all about good cloth. You're not doin' the job for the money, that's for sure, if you can afford quality like that!'

'Dr Barker is a friend of mine and I offered to help out while he's in hospital,' he replied evenly, shaking his head when Meg went to remonstrate with the old lady. 'And thank you for the compliment. It's nice to know I wasn't ripped off. Anyway, tell me about Sidney. How long were you married?'

It was just the opening Elsie needed. Meg Parker rolled her eyes as the old lady launched into her life story, muttering something about fetching Stephen a cup of tea as he'd need it. Elsie was still happily prattling away when she returned a quarter of an hour later, but Stephen knew only too well that the most important medicine of all for elderly patients was often the simplest—someone to listen to them.

He drank his tea, and when it looked as though Elsie was running out of steam he put his cup down and got round to the reason for his visit. 'It's been fascinating, hearing all that, Mrs Jones. But I'd better get on with what I'm here for otherwise Sister Parker might not let me come again. Can I take a look at your feet to see how they're coming along? I believe you had surgery about six weeks ago?'

'That's right.' Elsie slipped her feet out of the comfortable old slippers she was wearing. 'Bin a lot better, too, they 'ave. Not 'alf as painful.'

'Good. I'm glad to hear it.' Stephen carefully examined the area between the first metatarsal joint and the adjoining phalanx at the base of each of the old lady's big toes, and was pleased with what he found. The operation had done a great deal to correct the problem. Bunions were extremely painful and he was pleased that the old lady had gained some relief from the treatment.

'Well, that looks fine to me, Mrs Jones. Another couple of weeks and you should be ready to hit the dance floor again,' he teased as he helped her on with her slippers.

'If that's an offer then I accept!' The old lady sighed sadly. 'I used to be real light on me feet, I did, when I was a girl. My Sidney used to say as 'e'd never danced with anyone as light as me.'

'I'm sure you were, Elsie,' Meg cut in quickly before the old lady could set off on one of her tales again. 'Now, if you're ready, Dr Spencer…'

Stephen took the hint and stood up. He smiled at the old lady as he picked up his case. 'Maybe I'll see you again, Mrs Jones. I'll be here for the next six weeks so you never know.'

'In that case, you can come to me birthday party. Can't 'e, Sister?' Elsie didn't wait for confirmation. 'Next month it is. I'll be seventy-eight. I'll save you the first dance!'

'I'll keep you to that!' Stephen replied, laughing as he quickly followed Meg from the room. She paused to let him catch up with her and gave him a teasing smile.

'Looks as though you've made a big hit there. Elsie is quite smitten!'

'She's a wonderful old lady, isn't she?' Stephen replied, glancing over his shoulder.

'She is. You'd never believe the hard life she's had. She brought up ten children, six of her own plus four of her sister's after she died. Salt of the earth our Elsie is,' Meg said admiringly. 'It's people like her who make working in this job so rewarding. They have such a gutsy attitude to life.'

She started along the corridor that led to the bedrooms. Stephen followed her, taking note of how bright and cheerful the place looked. There were colourful prints on the walls and vases of flowers on every window-sill, which added to the homely atmosphere.

'Have you worked here long?' he asked.

'Coming up to ten years now.' Meg smiled at him over her shoulder. 'Never thought I'd stay that long when I first took the job. It was more of a stopgap, to be honest, before I moved onto something else. Geriatric care wasn't something I'd really considered, but I found myself enjoying the work more and more so I stayed. Of course, having people like Graham to turn to in a time of crisis has helped enormously. He's been marvellous.'

There was no mistaking the warm appreciation in her voice as she mentioned Graham's name. Stephen found himself wondering if Meg would like to share more than just a working relationship with his old friend. The suspicion grew stronger when she suddenly stopped and turned to him with real concern on her face.

'How is he, Dr Spencer? I rang the hospital but all I got was the usual meaningless stuff that he was as well as could be expected.' Meg coloured and looked away. 'I was wondering about visiting him but I wasn't sure if I should or not.'

'I'm sure Graham would love to see you,' Stephen replied enthusiastically, hoping he was right. Graham had never shown any inclination to form a relationship with another woman since his wife had died many years previously, but maybe it was time he thought about it. To Stephen's mind, Meg Parker would be the ideal candidate!

'I'll be going in to see him tomorrow so I'll let him know you want to pop in, shall I?' he offered, then changed the subject, sensing that it would be best not to press the point. 'Right, it's Mr Dickinson next, I believe. Chronic bronchitis, isn't it?'

They carried on with the visits but Stephen made a note to have a word with Alex when he got a chance to see if she knew the lie of the land, so to speak…

He gave an inward chuckle. He'd never thought he'd resort to matchmaking! This job was turning into something more than he'd expected in many ways!

By the time evening surgery came to an end, Stephen was exhausted. Not since his days as a junior hospital doctor had he worked so hard. He hadn't realised what a charmed life he'd been leading for the past few years if this was what NHS work amounted to.

Alex was on the telephone when he went to the office so he quietly said goodnight to Dorothy and went through to the house. He went straight up to his room and shed his suit in favour of jeans and a T-shirt then went down to the kitchen to see what there was to eat. Lunch had been a sandwich bought on his way back from the hospital and he was starving.

His hand hovered over the bacon before he forced himself to select something more healthy. A chicken breast with a selection of vegetables which could be stir-fried fitted the bill, and would be quick as well. He was just slicing the chicken into strips when Alex appeared.

'Want some? There's plenty for two,' he offered immediately, but she shook her head.

'No, it's fine. You carry on.' She went to the fridge and took out a wedge of cheese, cutting off a chunk before selecting an apple from the fruit bowl. Leaning against the worktop, she watched as he deftly sliced mushrooms and celery, then added strips of bright red pepper to the growing pile on the chopping board.

'Is that all you're going to have?' he asked, glancing at her sideways with a frown.

'I'm fine…really. How did you get on at the hospital with Danny?' she asked quickly, obviously not appreciating his concern about her eating habits. She bit into the apple, as though daring him to pass any further comment.

Stephen took the hint. It was up to her what she ate, of course, but to his mind it seemed downright silly to pass up the offer of a decent meal just to make a point!

'OK,' he said evenly, reaching for a bulb of garlic. He crushed a couple of cloves with the blade of the knife, releasing the pungent aroma into the room, then added the pulp to the rest of the vegetables. 'They agreed to do the scan in the end.'

'That sounds as though they were reluctant in the first place. Was there a problem about it?' Alex asked, frowning. She took another massive bite of apple, setting loose a fine spray of juice. She blushed as Stephen ran the back of his hand over his cheek to wipe away the traces of it. 'Sorry.'

'Don't worry. You're having to put up with the smell of my garlic so a drop of apple juice isn't going to cause any lasting damage,' he assured her with a teasing grin, which drew a hesitant smile from her.

She hurriedly finished her apple then bent to drop the core into the waste bin under the sink. Stephen just happened to turn round at that moment and he found his thoughts racing back to the previous night when he had watched her do much the same thing.

The demure grey skirt was no match for the jeans, he decided sadly, then gulped as he was suddenly treated to a tantalising glimpse of slender thigh as she bent over to retrieve something which had rolled to the back of the cupboard.

He hastily averted his eyes, reminding himself sternly about peeping Toms and voyeurs, and other such unsavoury characters, but it didn't make a scrap of difference as his imagination ran riot once more.

'Evidently, the scanner wasn't being used today. It seems the radiographer is on holiday and her replacement only works part time,' he said quickly, to give his mind something else to think about. 'I had to insist that they call in the relief operator, and I don't think the powers that be were too pleased.'

'I can imagine!' Alex agreed wryly. 'It costs money to run the scanner and there's never enough to go round.'

'Pretty pointless, having the equipment, if it lies idle, though,' he replied tartly, chancing another glance over his shoulder and pleased to see that Alex was standing upright once more. He'd never thought of himself as lecherous but that's how he seemed to react around her! Odd, when he thought about the other women he'd spent time with, and in far more intimate situations, yet he couldn't recall his imagination running away with him the way it kept doing at the moment.

'Oh, I agree.' She seemed mercifully unaware of his predicament as she continued. 'Although, in all fairness, if it was down to the medical staff there wouldn't be a problem. Unfortunately, a lot of these decisions are taken by the accountants and it's difficult to make them see past the pound signs at times. I imagine it was a rude awakening for you.'

'What do you mean?' he queried with a frown.

'That you probably don't come up against that kind of problem in your own practice. If one of your patients needs a scan they pay for it. There's no question of them being refused, is there?'

'No.' His tone was curt because he wasn't comfortable with the idea, although what she'd said was perfectly true. Suddenly, it seemed wrong that treatment should be withheld because a patient couldn't pay for it directly.

Why hadn't he really thought about it before? he wondered as he carried on slicing vegetables. Because he had become too comfortable in his own affluent world and forgotten that not everyone had access to the resources his patients took for granted? Or had he *deliberately* closed his mind to the realities of life because he hadn't wanted to think about them? He sensed that was closer to the truth and it didn't sit well with him.

'Did Debbie tell you about Graham's fight to get Danny onto genetically engineered Factor VIII?' Alex asked, grimacing as she tossed the mouldy apple core she had retrieved from the cupboard into the bin.

Stephen shrugged as he glanced at her, still uncomfortable with the idea that he had been deliberately burying his head in the sand because it had been easier on his conscience. 'No, she never mentioned it. I suppose she was too upset to give it much thought. Why? What's the story?' He put the knife down on the board as he turned to face her.

Alex sighed. 'You know there's always a small risk involved when using Factor VIII derived from donor blood?'

'I know that there used to be,' he countered. 'Hepatitis and Aids were both real dangers at one time. But all blood products are heat-treated nowadays, which reduces any risks to a minimum, although I do agree that it's far safer to use genetically engineered Factor VIII.'

He frowned. 'Are you saying there's been a problem about Danny having it?'

'Exactly. Graham has tried his best to persuade the area health authority to provide the extra funding but they won't be budged.' Her tone was grim. 'The cost of the genetically engineered product is much higher, you see, and their argument is that if they allow Danny to have it then every patient with haemophilia will want it. There isn't enough money in the budget, or so they claim.'

'That's disgraceful! We're talking about a child's long-term health here.' Stephen couldn't hide his concern. 'Even if the risks *are* small there's no point in taking them if there's a safer alternative.'

'I know. Debbie read an article about the genetically engi-neeered product in a magazine and naturally asked Graham if Danny could have it. He's done his best but…' Alex shrugged. 'If he'd been feeling fitter I'm sure he would have put up a better fight to persuade them, but he simply hasn't been up to taking them on.'

'Maybe I can do something about it,' Stephen said thought-fully. 'It's worth a try.'

'Is it?' She laughed shortly. 'Come on, Stephen, what point is there in you getting involved? You're only here for a few weeks and then you'll be leaving. Hardly seems worth both-ering, does it?'

She swung round to wash her hands, obviously considering that the end of the matter. Stephen wasn't deaf to the scathing note that had been in her voice, although he wasn't sure why his offer should have elicited such a response. It annoyed him all the more, coming on top of the realisation that he might have been avoiding certain issues in the past few years. He was just about to ask her for an explanation when she turned on the tap.

Water gushed out, hitting the edge of the washing-up bowl so that a fountain cascaded across the kitchen and caught him squarely in the centre of his chest.

'What the devil…?' he exclaimed, staring down at the soak-ing patch on the front of his clean T-shirt. He looked up in surprise when he heard what sounded suspiciously like a giggle issuing from Alex's direction. His brows knitted together in a frown as he saw the trouble she was having, keeping her face straight.

'I'm sorry…' She couldn't go on as she dissolved into gales of laughter. Pressing a hand to her mouth, she strove for com-posure. 'I didn't mean that to happen, honestly…'

Once again laughter got the better of her. Stephen shot an-other look down at his sopping shirt front. 'So you think it's funny, do you?' he asked in a voice that made her eyes wing to his face.

'I...uh...' She almost succeeded but once again laughter overcame her. 'Yes!'

Stephen wasn't sure what prompted him to make the next move—it certainly wasn't one he would have made if he'd been thinking logically. But there was something infectious about hearing her laugh like that because he sensed that it was rare for her to give in to amusement so wholeheartedly.

He gave her a slow, deliberate smile as he took a step forward so that she was trapped in the narrow gap between him and the sink unit.

'Wh-what are you doing?' There was the faintest hint of uncertainty in her voice now, but it wasn't enough to disguise the amusement that still lingered. Stephen grinned wolfishly, his gaze going deliberately to the running water.

'No... Oh, no! It was an accident. Honestly! Stephen...' Her voice rose to a shriek as he reached past her and scooped up a handful of cold water. Her eyes were huge as they flew to his while she waited to see what punishment he intended to mete out. Her lips parted on a tiny gasp of surprise as he let a single cold drop trickle down her cheek...

Stephen wasn't sure when the mood shifted. One minute he was preparing to give Alex a taste of her own medicine and the next the mood had switched so fast that he barely had time to realise what was happening.

He took a deep breath but it did nothing to ease the tension which had beset him. Every muscle in his body seemed to be strung so tight that he couldn't move as he stood there, watching the droplet of water sliding down her cheek.

'Stephen...' Her voice held neither amusement nor uncertainty now, yet what it did hold seemed to release him from the spell. Water pooled on the floor as he opened his fingers but he didn't notice it. His hand had something far more important to do now than teach her a lesson...

The feel of her skin was a revelation as he let his fingers follow the shimmering path the droplet had left on her cheek. He wasn't sure why but he'd expected it to feel cold to the touch, yet it was so warm and soft, so smooth and velvety, that he couldn't seem to get enough of touching it.

He laid his palm flat against her cheek, hearing the murmur she gave, yet he knew instinctively that it stemmed from pleasure, not protest. That thought was the most delicious stimulant to senses already heightened to an almost unbearable degree.

His fingers curled beneath the lobe of her ear so that he could feel the delicacy of the bones in her neck through their tips, feel how the silken wisps of hair which had escaped from her chignon tickled his knuckles, how her pulse was beating so enticingly beneath his thumb…

He wasn't aware that he had started to bend towards her, hadn't even formed the thought that he was going to kiss her, when the sound of the doorbell broke the spell. Alex gave a sharp gasp, like a swimmer breaking the surface after being under water too long.

'Th-that will be Simon.' Her voice was husky and she cleared her throat. 'He…he said he would drop by tonight to tell me how Graham is, maybe bring a take-away…'

She trailed off uncertainly but she'd said more than enough. Stephen stepped back, feeling mercifully numb. Maybe he would feel something later—shock, anger, even regret at his own stupidity—but at that moment he simply felt empty. 'You'd better let him in, then, hadn't you?'

'I… Yes. Of course.' She hurried from the room and Stephen heard the sound of voices which faded abruptly as the sitting-room door closed.

He turned back to the chopping board but his appetite had disappeared along with his emotions. He slid the vegetables into a plastic bag and re-wrapped the chicken, then put every-thing back in the fridge, before leaving the kitchen. He went back down the hall, deliberately quickening his pace as he passed the sitting-room. He wouldn't allow himself to think about what was happening in there any more than he intended to dwell on what had happened just now in the kitchen. Some things were best forgotten for everyone's sake!

CHAPTER FIVE

'AM I right in thinking that you'll be going to see Graham this afternoon?'

Stephen paused in the doorway to Alex's room, fixing a neutral expression to his face as she looked up from the notes she'd been writing. It was two days since the incident in the kitchen and they'd treated one another with such courtesy that Emily Post would have been impressed!

He felt sudden impatience as he watched her smooth her features into an equally noncommittal expression. This was getting ridiculous! They couldn't keep on tiptoeing around each other all the time. Maybe it had seemed best to try to forget what had happened but it obviously wasn't working. But deciding how to clear the air was another matter entirely. Would apologising for the fact that he'd *nearly* kissed her really be such a good idea?

'I thought I'd pop in to see him after I've finished at the baby clinic. I'm on call tonight so I won't be able to go then.' Alex's tone was as bland as her expression but, then, she'd never had any difficulty behaving that way around him, Stephen acknowledged wryly. She gave him a chillingly polite smile. 'Do you want me to give him a message?'

'Sort of.' He shrugged, trying not to let her see how that last thought had stung. 'Meg Parker mentioned something about wanting to visit him. I promised her that I'd find out if it was all right, but I forgot to ask Graham when I saw him. Maybe you could mention it? I got the feeling that Meg was...well, rather fond of him.'

Alex laughed softly as she leaned back in her chair. 'So you get that impression, too, do you? I've had my suspicions for a while that Meg is just a little bit in love with Graham.'

'Mmm, so I wasn't that far off track?' Stephen mused as he leaned against the doorframe and regarded her quizzically. 'And how does Graham feel? Any idea?'

'I don't think he's noticed, to be frank.' Alex sighed as she tossed her pen onto the blotter then stretched her arms above her head. The action caused her pale blue blouse to work free of the waistband of her navy skirt so that Stephen caught a glimpse of smooth, bare midriff before she sank back into the chair.

He took a deep breath, struggling to control the sudden quickening of awareness that ran through his body. He had to stop this! So Alex *was* a beautiful and desirable woman but she was first and foremost a colleague. Simple ethics demanded that he kept that to the forefront of his mind!

He dragged his thoughts back into line as he realised she was speaking, mentally filling in the bits he'd missed.

'…seemed interested. I believe he was married, wasn't he?' She paused and he hurried to answer the question.

'He was. His wife died many years ago, though, before Graham started this practice, so I don't remember her.' He shrugged. 'And you're right that Graham has never seemed interested in another relationship. I think work has filled any gaps in his life, but maybe it's time he started thinking about himself for a change. He isn't that far away from retirement.'

'He won't retire until he can hand over the reins to someone he knows he can trust.'

Stephen frowned at the certainty in her voice. 'That sounds as though you've discussed it with him. Have you?'

'Less a discussion than a simple deduction.' Her gaze was piercing all of a sudden. 'Did you know that the area health authority is thinking about building a health centre for this community? They've written to Graham a number of times, outlining their proposals and asking for his views.'

'No, I didn't know that.' Stephen frowned. 'Surely he isn't against the idea? It would be the best thing all round—new facilities, new equipment, definitely more doctors to staff the place. It's obvious that this practice is overstretched at present.'

'Oh, Graham is all for the idea.' She pushed back her chair with sudden impatience. 'You, better than anyone, should know that the only thing he's interested in is making sure this community gets the best medical service available.'

'But?' He laughed shortly, wondering why it suddenly felt as though *he'd* done something to annoy her. 'There was a definite reservation to that statement, Alex. So, come on, out with it.'

'*But* Graham wants to be sure that the right person is put in charge of the new centre. He's worried sick that it will be staffed by doctors who don't have any real interest in this community. Realistically, he knows he won't be able to take on the position himself in his state of health. But he's been stalling the health authority until he gets their assurance that he can have his say on who will run the place,' she informed him tersely.

'And has he someone in mind?' Stephen asked apprehensively, because he had a horrible suspicion that he knew where the conversation was leading.

'I think that's something you need to discuss with Graham, don't you?' She picked up her jacket from the back of her chair and headed for the door. She turned to look back and there was a tightness to the smile she gave him. 'Unfortunately, he seems to have made up his mind, and neither my views nor anyone else's will make him see that he's making a big mistake.'

She left the room and Stephen heard the hall door slam a few seconds later. He ran his hand through his hair, feeling as though he'd just been poleaxed.

Did Graham want *him* to take over as director of the new health centre? Was that what he was hoping for? Surely not!

Stephen tried to convince himself that he was on the wrong track but it was impossible to dismiss the idea now that it had been planted in his mind. He quickly ran through all the reasons he couldn't take on the job, first and foremost being that he didn't want it! He had his own practice, which he certainly wasn't prepared to give up. Nor had he any intention of coming back to this area to work on a permanent basis when his main aim all along had been to escape from it!

He let out a sigh of relief once he'd listed his objections and found them watertight. Graham must know how he'd feel about the idea, too, so it *couldn't* be him Graham had in mind for the job. Alex had got it wrong. She'd admitted that Graham hadn't discussed it with her, so she'd probably added two and two and come up with *his* name as the prospective candidate. She certainly hadn't made any secret of how she felt about the idea, however!

Stephen's mouth compressed as he left the room. He collected the list of calls for that afternoon then left the surgery. Getting into his car, he started the engine with a roar that hinted at his displeasure. Alex Campbell had judged him unfit for the post after what—three days' acquaintance? It made no difference that he didn't want the damned job—it still annoyed him intensely. The downright cheek of the woman! Just who did she think she was to find *him* lacking?

Stephen had calmed down by the time he parked in front of Eden House. Danny was first on his list, although this was the last day he would need to give the boy an injection. The cuts on the child's face were healing nicely, and although the bruising on his hip was still very painful it wasn't getting any worse. The injections of Factor VIII had worked their usual magic.

He set the car alarm then headed for the entrance to the tower block, pausing as a couple of teenage boys came out just at that moment. They looked him up and down, taking an obvious interest in the case he was carrying. Stephen stared straight back at them, not at all intimidated by the hostile expressions on their faces. He hadn't been away from the area long enough to forget the first basic rule: act like a victim and you'd soon become one!

'Come on, Jace, let's get a move on.' The taller of the two, a boy with straggling fair hair, nudged his friend sharply in the ribs and they headed off across the car park. Stephen stayed where he was until he was sure they had gone, before going inside. He'd bet a pound to a penny they were up to no good but there wasn't a lot he could do about it.

Danny was watching a programme on TV when Stephen was shown into the flat. He sat down on the settee and accepted the cup of tea Debbie offered him.

'Thanks. I could do with this. So, how are you feeling today, Danny?' he asked, putting the cup and saucer down to open his case and take out a syringe.

'OK, I suppose.'

The flat note in the boy's voice was unmistakable and Stephen raised his brows questioningly at Debbie, who sighed.

'He's bored with being stuck in here all the time,' she explained. 'He misses his friends from school.'

'Oh, I see. Still, you'll be well enough to go back next week. Right, you know the routine so go to it!' Stephen waited while Danny rolled up his sleeve for the injection. The child screwed his eyes tightly shut so that he couldn't see the needle going into his arm.

'Is it done now?' he asked, peeping through slitted lids as Stephen finished.

'Yes. And that's the last one you'll need,' Stephen assured him as he started to clear everything away.

'I wish I never had to have another one!' Danny muttered belligerently. 'I hate being like this. It isn't fair!'

'It isn't. Unfortunately, there isn't anything we can do about it, Danny. I only wish there was.' Stephen snapped his case shut, saddened to see tears in the child's eyes. 'Still, with a bit of luck you won't need any more injections for a while, eh?' he added encouragingly.

'It still doesn't mean I can be the same as everyone else, though! I'm fed up, not being able to go out and play with my friends.' Danny got up and rushed from the room, obviously upset.

'I'm sorry about that, Dr Spencer,' Debbie apologised, but Stephen shook his head.

'Don't worry about it. It's only natural that he should get upset at times. Watching his friends doing all the things he wants to do, it can't be easy at his age.'

'It isn't.' Debbie sighed as she wiped a few tears from her own eyes. 'He's usually so good about it but I think what happened gave him a real scare. He's been very subdued these past few days, as though it's been praying on his mind.'

'Has he said who hit him yet and why?' Stephen asked, frowning.

'No. I think he's too frightened to tell me. Obviously, whoever it was threatened him not to say anything. But I have my own ideas,' she added grimly. 'Most of the trouble round here is caused by the Richardson boys, and by the eldest boy, Darren, in particular. He's a really nasty piece of work. It was him and a couple of his friends who terrorised Neelam's daughter and son-in-law. That's why they're living next door with her, because they're too afraid to go home to their own flat. Evidently, Darren threatened to do something to their baby.'

'And weren't the police informed?' Stephen asked grimly. 'Something like that needs looking into before it gets out of hand.'

'People are afraid to say anything. The police do their best but the Richardsons always have an alibi, so it ends up that the police can't charge them with anything.' Debbie shrugged. 'They get even nastier if they think people have been telling tales on them.'

'I still think something should be done. Have you thought

about forming a residents' committee? It would be easier to take a stand that way because everyone could work together as a team,' he suggested.

'Sort of safety in numbers, you mean?' Debbie frowned thoughtfully. 'It's a good idea. I'll try suggesting it to a few people around here and see what they think. Neelam should be home from hospital soon, so I'll have a word with her...through Darla if we get stuck,' she explained when Stephen's brows rose. She laughed. 'Although it's amazing how much we can talk about even with the language barrier!'

Stephen laughed at that. 'Where there's a will there's a way, eh? Anyway, I'm glad that Mrs Bashir has made such good progress. I was speaking to her consultant only this morning and he said that he was delighted with the way she's responded to treatment. I expect you'll be pleased to have her back. How have you managed about work?'

Debbie sighed as she saw him to the door. 'I had to take time off because I couldn't leave Danny. They promised to keep my job open so I'm keeping my fingers crossed that's what they've done. I clean at one of the big office blocks on the dock road. I work from four till seven each morning,' she explained.

Stephen hid a grimace. Hardly the best hours for a woman caring for a child. However, he diplomatically didn't say anything because he doubted that Debbie would have chosen to do the job unless she needed the money desperately.

He sighed as he made his way down in the lift. It reminded him of how his own mother had struggled when he'd been a child, taking on any job she could find to put food on the table and keep a roof over their heads. Women like her and Debbie deserved medals for the way they coped!

Graham was sitting up in bed, looking extremely cheerful, when Stephen popped in to see him that evening after surgery finished. He was making steady progress as he recovered from the operation, and Stephen was delighted to see that he seemed to be regaining a lot of his old vigour.

He smiled as he set the stack of magazines he'd brought on the bedside locker, making space for them alongside a brand-new hardback novel. 'Well, no need to ask how you are, Graham. You're looking fine!'

'I feel fine. Fitter than I've felt in ages, to be honest.' Graham sighed ruefully. 'I only wish I'd had the good sense to have the operation done months ago.'

Stephen frowned as he sat down, suddenly reminded of what Alex had said that morning. 'So why didn't you?' he asked, trying a bit of gentle probing although he was ninety-nine per cent certain that she'd been wrong. 'Was it just because of the problems of finding a locum? Or was there another reason?'

Graham shifted uncomfortably. 'Oh, you know how it is. There's so much to do that you keep putting things off. Anyway, it's done now, and with a bit of luck I'll be out of here by the end of next week.'

It was obvious that he didn't intend to say anything more so Stephen didn't pursue it. Graham would tell him his plans in his own time, although it was unlikely that he himself featured in them, as Alex suspected. Stephen pushed the nagging worry to the back of his mind as he ran through a carefully edited version of what had been happening at the surgery.

'So you've no need to worry,' he concluded. 'We're rubbing along just fine without you, although every patient I see asks how you are and when you'll be back. It doesn't do a lot for the ego to know you're second best, I can tell you!'

Graham laughed at that. 'There's nothing second best about the treatment folk are receiving from you and Alex! The pair of you make a first-rate team, I'll bet.'

Stephen smiled noncommittally, deeming it wiser not to say anything. How would Graham feel if he knew that Alex was far less keen on Stephen working in the practice than he'd anticipated? Stephen could guess only too well, and the last thing he wanted was for Graham to start worrying.

He stood up when a nurse popped her head round the door to remind him not to stay too long. 'I'd better go. I'll come again soon, though. Is there anything you need?'

Graham shook his head. 'No, I've got everything, thanks.' He glanced at the bedside cabinet and chuckled. 'I'm certainly being spoilt! Meg popped in just before you arrived and she brought me the latest Dick Francis novel. It will be a real treat, having time just to lie here and read.'

'Meg Parker, do you mean? She mentioned something about visiting you.' Stephen hid a smile as he saw the decidedly bashful expression on Graham's face.

'Oh…um, yes. She said she'd seen you and that you were a big hit at the nursing home,' Graham replied, hurriedly turning the conversation to what had gone on at Arden House.

Stephen left shortly afterwards. He went out to his car, still smiling to himself. Maybe he and Alex had been wrong about Graham not having noticed Meg's interest, he thought ruefully. There had been a look in his old friend's eyes just now which had hinted at that, and at the fact that Graham might reciprocate Meg's feelings! Things were definitely looking up in that area. He would have to tell Alex about it when he got back—

He cut that thought dead. Perhaps it would be wiser to confine their conversations to purely professional matters both in and out of work. Anything else seemed to lead to situations neither of them were comfortable with.

That led him squarely back to what had happened in the kitchen and he sighed as he started the engine. Not again!

It was gone eleven when Stephen got back to the house. He had stopped off to see a film, instead of going straight back, then had had something to eat afterwards. He'd felt that he'd needed a bit of breathing space but the evening hadn't been as successful as he'd hoped.

Too many times he'd found his thoughts turning to Alex as he'd wondered what she was doing—if she'd eaten properly or just made herself the usual snack, whether she'd been called out, even whether Simon Ross had paid her another visit. Now he sighed as he turned into the drive.

What was it about the wretched woman that got to him like this? He couldn't recall anyone ever having taken up so much of his thoughts. Was it just that he was having difficulty coming to terms with the fact that she seemed to dislike him so much?

It was an explanation of sorts, although he wasn't sure it was the real reason. However, he had to admit to feeling relieved when he saw that her car wasn't parked in its customary spot and realised that she must have been called out. At least he wouldn't have to go through another meaningless polite conversation!

He was in bed, reading an article in one of the medical journals he subscribed to, when he heard the sound of a car engine. He turned over the page, forcing himself to concentrate. The article was about the effects of pollutants on children suffering from asthma and there was a lot that was relevant to what he had seen recently. However, he found it increasingly difficult to concentrate as he kept listening for the front door to open.

After a full ten minutes had passed and there was still no sound of movement downstairs he got out of bed and went to the window. His room overlooked the drive and he quickly spotted Alex's car parked in its usual place. It was quite dark outside so that it was difficult to see clearly but he could have sworn that she was still sitting inside it.

He felt the first stirrings of alarm as he grabbed his robe and hurried downstairs, switching on the hall light so that he could see as he went out to the car. His fear intensified as he got closer and saw how she was slumped over the steering-wheel.

Without stopping to think, he hauled open the car door, then cursed himself as he heard her startled cry. 'It's all right,' he said quickly. 'It's me, Alex…Stephen.'

'Stephen?' For a moment he wondered if she recognised him because there was such bewilderment in her voice.

'What's happened, sweetheart? Tell me.' Instinctively, his tone gentled and he saw her take a shuddering breath.

'Two boys…teenagers…outside Adam House…' She couldn't go on but he had already caught the drift of what she was trying to tell him. He felt a surge of fury run through his veins and had to struggle not to show any sign of it as he reached into the car and gently pried her fingers off the steering-wheel.

'Let's get you inside then you can tell me the whole story. Come along now.' He slid his arm round her waist as he urged her out of the car, feeling the tremor which shook her from head to toe. His expression was murderous as his mind ran riot with thoughts of what might have gone on.

Sitting her down at the kitchen table, he went to the sink and filled a glass with water then took it back to her. 'Take a sip of this…slowly now.'

The glass rattled against her teeth because she was shaking so hard. Stephen took it from her, holding it while she took a couple of tiny sips. She shook her head when he offered it to her once more. 'No more…thank you.'

Even now she clung to courtesy but Stephen sensed it was because she was afraid that she would break down otherwise. He put the glass on the table then sat down opposite her, taking hold of her cold hands to chafe them between his. 'Can you tell me what happened, Alex?' he prompted gently. 'You said something about two boys…?'

For a second her fingers gripped his before she forced herself to relax, yet she didn't draw her hands away as he might have expected her to. He had the feeling that she found his touch reassuring and couldn't describe the pleasure he felt at that thought.

'I had to go out on a call to Adam House, a baby with a bad case of croup, as it turned out.' Her voice was toneless as she recited the events of the night. 'Donna, the baby's mother, is only seventeen and she's on her own. I could tell that she was scared so I stayed until I was sure that the child was all right. There was nobody about when I came out of the building so I went straight to my car. I was just about to get in when these two boys appeared…'

She stopped. Stephen gave her a moment to compose herself then gently urged her to tell the rest of the tale. 'So then what happened, Alex? Can you tell me?'

She took a deep breath. 'They came running towards me. I didn't know what they wanted at first. Then one of them made a grab for my case but—and don't ask me how—I managed to hold onto it. The other boy started swearing and pushed me so hard that I fell over. I was still holding onto my bag because I realised that was what they were after and I didn't want them to get their hands on the contents. I don't know what would have happened only just at that moment a car came into the car park and they ran off.'

She eased her hands free to wipe away the tears that were streaming down her face. 'I was so scared, Stephen…'

She couldn't go on as a sob racked her. Stephen was out of his seat in a flash. Kneeling down beside her chair, he drew her into his arms and held her while she sobbed.

'Shh. It's all right. There's nothing to be frightened of now. I'm here. And I won't let anything happen to you,' he murmured, struggling against the anger he felt. If he ever got his hands on whoever had done this to her…!

He forced himself to relax as he stroked her hair, feeling its silken softness clinging to his fingers. It had worked loose from its chignon so that as he drew her head against his shoulder the last few pins fell out.

Stephen felt his breath catch as it rippled down her back. He hadn't realised before just how long it was, or that once it had been freed from the severe style she favoured it would twist itself into such a glorious tangle of curls. He was completely mesmerised by the sight.

'I'm sorry. I'm making such a fool of myself...' She took a shaky breath as she drew back to look at him. 'I...I don't normally go to pieces like this.'

'You don't *normally* get terrorised in the line of duty so I don't think it's an indication that you're going soft in your old age,' he teased, and earned himself a watery smile.

'Less of the "old", thank you,' she retorted with a trace of her former spirit.

'Sorry. I didn't mean to touch a nerve.' He laughed as she gasped in outrage, pleased to see that she was starting to look a little better. 'I was just teasing. Honestly!'

He stood up and plugged in the kettle, not sure that he could trust himself to remain close to her any longer as she gave him another hesitant smile. The urge to take her in his arms and kiss away the last traces of fear was very strong but that was the last thing he should do. He would never forgive himself if he took advantage of the situation!

'Did you phone the police and tell them what happened?' he asked in a voice which grated with the effort it cost him not to give in to the urge.

It was odd how she awoke all sorts of primitive responses he'd never known he possessed before. Although he had the usual healthy interest in the female of the species, he had never had trouble controlling his appetites. He enjoyed sex and enjoyed being with a woman, but he had never felt this sort of *hunger* he felt around her. It shocked him that he should feel this deeply when he had always been so in control of his emotions in the past.

'No. I should have done, of course, but I just wanted to get back here.' She looked down at the tissue she was shredding. 'I keep thinking of what might have happened if that car hadn't come along...'

'But it did come, Alex. I know how scared you must have been but try not to let your mind run away with you.' It was easy to give the advice but he guessed how hard it was going to be for her to take it. He felt a sudden angry impatience at the thought of the danger she'd been in.

'Frankly, you shouldn't have been there on your own at this time of night! I don't know what Graham has been thinking of, letting you put yourself at risk like that.'

Her head came up at that and there was no mistaking the haughty glitter in her eyes. 'What are you suggesting, Stephen? That I play on the fact that I'm a woman to get out of doing my fair share of the work around here?'

'No. What I'm saying is that *nobody* should be put at risk that way. It's foolish when it can be avoided by taking a few simple precautions,' he retorted, disliking her tone. Didn't she understand that he was only concerned about her welfare? Apparently not!

'There's no way that Graham would agree to buy in a night-time on-call service. And no way I would expect him to,' she stated bluntly. 'Maybe you're a little out of touch with how the real world operates, Stephen. Not everyone has access to the kind of resources you're used to. Every penny coming into this practice is accounted for. There simply isn't enough in the budget to pay for unnecessary luxuries!'

'I'd argue the point about it being "unnecessary" to ensure your safety, Alex, only obviously now isn't the best time to discuss it rationally.' He heard the condescending note in his voice but made no apology for it. Her stubborn refusal to see sense infuriated him. Would she have listened to someone else, like Simon Ross, for instance?

He wasn't sure what sort of a relationship Alex had with Ross—she certainly hadn't given him any clue about it. But just the thought that she might have accepted the suggestion from the other man more readily than she had from *him* did little to cool his temper.

She got to her feet with a scraping of chair legs against tiles which made him wince. 'Then there doesn't seem any point in continuing this conversation, does there? Thank you, Dr Spencer. I appreciate the concern you showed me tonight.'

She didn't exactly flounce out of the room—that would have been quite out of character. However, the effect was much the same. Stephen swore under his breath but his anger was turned inwards rather than directed at her.

A fine mess he'd made of that! What was the matter with him? Until a few days ago he'd considered himself capable of dealing with any problem calmly and rationally, yet a few minutes' discussion with Alex and he started trying to lay down the law!

He switched off the kettle then turned to go back upstairs, only to come to a halt as he found her in the doorway. For a moment neither of them said anything, then she took a quick breath before the words came tumbling out.

'I'm sorry I snapped like that. I know that you were only trying to help.' She gave a small shrug, her brow wrinkling in confusion. 'I don't normally go off the deep end like that. I suppose it must have been the fright I had.'

You and me both! Stephen thought ruefully, grasping the explanation she'd handed him because he didn't want to look too deeply into the reason he'd acted so out of character himself.

'And I'm sorry if I sounded rather, well, chauvinistic?' he offered, willing to do his bit.

She chuckled lightly. 'You did rather. But you're right about us needing to do something. I've never mentioned it to Graham but a few times I've felt a bit edgy when I've been out on a call at night, especially when the lifts haven't been working in one of the tower blocks. It can be quite unnerving, having to walk up all those stairs in the dark.'

'Unnerving and risky. There's no knowing who could be lying in wait for you,' he said tersely.

She shivered. 'Don't! It makes me feel all creepy, thinking about it. So what do you suggest? Graham would never agree to employing an on-call service permanently. He told me he only resorts to using them if it's a dire emergency. It's not just because of the cost either. He firmly believes that a patient should be able to see his own doctor, not a stranger, whenever he's ill.'

'Don't I know it?' Stephen smiled wryly. 'Graham instilled that into me, a sort of eleventh commandment!' He sighed as she laughed. 'Look, I'm not sure what the answer is but we're both agreed that something needs to be done, aren't we?'

'Yes. It's silly for any of us to take risks unnecessarily,' she agreed.

'It is.' He crossed the kitchen and smiled down at her. 'So, will you leave it to me to work something out, Alex?'

'Yes. All right.' Her voice sounded suddenly husky in the silence. There was only the ticking of the clock in the hall to be heard and that provided a gentle ambience. She looked up at him and suddenly grinned. 'Just don't come up with anything that will cost an arm and a leg, will you?'

He laughed at that, relieved that they'd managed to find a compromise. He didn't enjoy always being at odds with her. He would much prefer that they worked in some degree of harmony...

He quickly confined his wayward thoughts before they started straying again. 'Cross my heart and hope to die—is that good enough for you?'

'Oh, I think so!' She laughed. 'Let's shake on it.'

She held out her hand and Stephen took it. It seemed the most natural thing in the world to draw her towards him and kiss her on the cheek to seal the bargain...

There was a moment when neither of them moved. Stephen certainly didn't try to, namely because he couldn't. The feel of her velvety cheek beneath his lips seemed to have turned his limbs to stone. Only his heart seemed capable of movement, beating like crazy as it sent blood racing to places he couldn't recall having been aware of before.

How could toenails tingle? he wondered dizzily. And how could a kiss make every hair on his body throb? It defied all logic, not to mention everything he'd learned in anatomy classes!

He gave a muffled murmur, quickly turning it into a cough as Alex stepped back. He let go of her hand, praying that he didn't look as shaken as he felt. How could one kiss cause so much havoc? On the Richter scale it was a definite ten!

'It seems we have a bargain, then,' he said hoarsely, striving for just the right degree of nonchalance and missing the mark by yards.

'I...uh, yes. So it appears.' She paused, as though wondering if she should say anything else, before obviously thinking better of it and hurrying from the room.

Stephen heard her run upstairs then the sound of her bedroom door being firmly closed. He sighed, torn between relief that things hadn't gone any further and disappointment. He switched off the kitchen light, went straight to his room and got into bed. The magazine was still open at the page he'd been reading so he decided to finish the article.

It was only when he realised he'd read the same paragraph at least five times that he gave up and turned off the light. Quite frankly, his head was too full of thoughts of Alex to absorb anything else!

CHAPTER SIX

BY EIGHT o'clock the following morning Stephen felt as though he'd done a full day's work! He'd been up before six and had gone for a run, before telephoning the police station. The sergeant on duty had promised to send an officer round to the surgery to take a statement from Alex, although Stephen suspected from the man's tone that he didn't think it would achieve very much.

He was at his desk, reading through some notes, when Dorothy let herself into the surgery a short time later. She stopped by his door, her brows rising quizzically as she saw him.

'Who's an early bird, then? Couldn't you sleep, Stephen?' She gave him a long, hard look, taking note of the shadows under his eyes. 'Not a guilty conscience, I hope?'

Stephen laughed, as she'd intended him to, wishing the restless night could be put down to something so simple. Should he feel guilty that once again he'd spent it thinking about Alex? He wasn't sure but it was becoming a habit he dearly wished he could break!

'Speak for yourself,' he retorted, however, giving the elderly receptionist an easy smile. 'My conscience is perfectly clear, thank you very much!'

'Then it must be something else which has given you those bags under your eyes. Don't tell me you've been burning the midnight oil like you used to do,' she replied, glancing pointedly at the papers on the desk. 'I remember Dr Barker being really worried when you lived here. He used to tell me how you stayed up till all hours, poring over your textbooks. It's about time you found yourself a nice girl and started a family, Stephen. That would take your mind off work fast enough!'

'I'm sure it would. The trouble is that I haven't met anyone yet who can match up to you, Dorothy,' he teased.

'Oh, get on with you! You can't tell me that the women aren't falling over themselves to catch your eye,' she retorted. 'Surely there's at least one of them in with a chance?'

'If there is I haven't come across her,' he replied lightly, trying to dismiss the image of a woman with long red hair that sprang to mind. Could he really see Alex Campbell as his wife? No way! Oh, she was certainly beautiful and intelligent, but the fact that she didn't like him was a definite drawback.

He dismissed the thought, concentrating instead on something far more urgent than his love life, or lack of one. 'While you're here, Dorothy, can I pick your brains? We have a bit of a problem.'

He quickly outlined what had happened the previous night, assuring her that Alex was unharmed before getting down to what he planned to do about the situation. 'It seems to me that it's downright foolish for any of us to go out at night on our own and put ourselves at risk like that. Although we don't carry anything more than the basic drugs we need in the course of our work, a lot of people don't realise that.'

He sighed as he tilted his chair back and studied the cracks in the ceiling. 'I suspect those two boys were after drugs, you see. And that's why they wanted Alex's case.'

'I'm sure you're right,' Dorothy agreed sadly. 'There're a lot of youngsters around here who are taking stuff they shouldn't. My Rita only remarked on it the other day, said that she saw that Darren Richardson in the hallway to our flats and that he was up to no good.'

'You're not the first person to mention his name,' Stephen observed thoughtfully. 'Debbie Francis seems to think it was him who hit little Danny. Evidently, Darren has something of a reputation around here.'

'Him and the rest of the family. The whole lot are a disgrace. The kids run riot and neither the mother nor the father seem to care. Anyway, what are you going to do about this, Stephen? I take it you've got some sort of plan?'

Stephen nodded as he let the chair drop back onto all four legs. 'I have. I've decided that the best solution would be to hire a driver to accompany whoever is on duty each night. That's what the on-call services do, and it makes sense. I was wondering if you knew of anyone reliable who would be willing to work unsocial hours?'

'Barry Jones,' Dorothy suggested immediately. 'He lives in the next flat to us and he'd take the job like a shot and be glad of it. His wife's just had their first child, and Barry lost his job a couple of weeks ago so they're struggling to make ends meet. He'd be perfect, Stephen.'

'Great! Then would you mind having a word with him and ask him to pop in to see me as soon as he can?' Stephen asked, delighted to have found a likely candidate so quickly. 'I'd like him to start straight away, assuming that he's interested, of course.'

'I'll give him a call right now,' Dorothy assured him, hurrying away to do just that. He heard her stop to speak to someone and managed to compose his features into a suitable expression as Alex appeared, wishing he could control the thundering of his heart as well.

Why did it race like this at the mere sight of her? he wondered. It had never happened before and he wasn't sure why it should be happening now. All right, so he *was* attracted to her—what red-blooded male this side of a hundred wouldn't be? But did that really explain the way his pulse was racing now or how he'd felt last night? Could it be put down to good old-fashioned sexual attraction? The more he thought about it the less convinced he was, but he wasn't ready to look for an alternative just yet.

'Dorothy just told me about you wanting to hire a driver,'

Alex said as she came into the room. She was looking as fresh as a daisy as usual, the crisp lemon blouse she was wearing with a dark brown skirt as immaculate as ever. Only the shadows under her eyes hinted at the fact that she, too, had spent a restless night. Stephen found himself wondering if it had been due to the scare she'd had or something else, before he realised how foolish it was to start thinking along those lines.

'So what do you think? It seems the most logical solution to me.' He shrugged, determinedly focused on convincing her. 'With a driver to act as back-up, there won't be the same risk involved in attending a night-time call for any of us.'

'I think it's an excellent idea. My only reservation is how much it's going to cost.' She sighed as she smoothed a wisp of hair back into its chignon, immediately drawing his attention to the richness of its colour. He had a sudden mental flash of how she had looked the night before, with those lustrous waves tumbling around her shoulders, before he quickly edited it.

There's a time and a place, Stephen, he reminded himself, wishing he didn't need reminding all the time!

'Leave me to worry about that,' he said instead, gathering up the papers to slip them back into their folder. 'I'm sure Graham and I will be able to work things out once he's out of hospital.'

'Well, if you're sure…' She hesitated, a frown drawing her delicate eyebrows together as she saw what he'd been reading. 'Isn't that the correspondence Graham has had with the area health authority about Danny and the Factor VIII?'

'Mmm. I thought I'd glance through it to see what had been said.' Stephen shrugged as he put the folder back into the filing cabinet. 'The last time Graham was in contact with them about it was over two months ago.'

'He hasn't been well enough to cope with anything more than the basics recently,' Alex said a shade defensively.

'That wasn't meant as a criticism, merely an observation,' he said quietly. 'Dorothy told me how things have been around here for the past few months. I only wish I'd known about it sooner.'

'Why? What would you have done, Stephen? Given up your own lucrative practice to come here and take over? Oh, I know you've agreed to cover for the next few weeks, but after that it won't be your problem, will it?' She laughed sharply, a touch of colour rimming her elegant cheek-bones. 'You'll be able to go back to the suburbs, safe in the knowledge that you've done your bit!'

'Meaning, of course, that I should do more?' His tone was as biting as hers had been. He didn't appreciate being put on the defensive like this. Was that what lay behind her animosity towards him, that she didn't think he'd done enough to help Graham when he'd needed it most? The fact that Stephen's own conscience had been plaguing him did little to soothe his ruffled feelings.

'That's for you to decide, isn't it?' She turned to march out of the room but Stephen caught hold of her arm to stop her. His grey eyes shimmered as they searched her set face.

'What is it with you, Alex? What exactly are you getting at? Ever since I arrived you've done your best to make me feel guilty, but I'm not sure what I'm supposed to have done!'

'Don't you? Come on, Stephen, you're not stupid. You must know that Graham thinks the world of you. His conversation is peppered with ''Stephen has done so well'' or ''Nobody could have worked harder than Stephen has''! What Graham *doesn't* say, however, is how disappointed he is that making money is obviously more important to you than making a contribution to society!'

He couldn't believe what he was hearing. He didn't even stop to consider if what she'd said was true. Obviously, his supposed neglect of Graham was just the tip of the iceberg! It was his whole way of life that Alex found so distasteful, the way he'd fought his way to the top professionally, at least. Who the hell did she think she was to stand there and pass judgement on him?

His smile was so glacial that he felt the shiver that ran through her body. 'And only by working in this kind of a job can I make that contribution? Is that what you're saying—that the rich don't have needs as well? That when they're ill it isn't so bad because they have money to cushion them?'

He laughed scornfully as he let her go. 'Grow up, Alex! You're too old for adolescent fantasies. This is the real world we're living in and how I choose to live my life is my business!'

'Maybe it is. But are you happy, Stephen? Do you have everything you want in your life, money *and* job satisfaction?' She shrugged. 'Maybe you do. After all, why should you worry about those who live in a world you have no experience of?'

'By that you mean this world here?' His laughter was so bitter that it brought her eyes to his face, but suddenly he was beyond caring what she thought. His tone was like the snap of a whip, each word cutting through the silence.

'Oh, I know what it's like all right. I was born three streets away from this very surgery, Alex, in a house with no bathroom and just an outside toilet. I grew up surrounded by poverty and decay, by the sort of hopelessness that stems from knowing that nobody gives a damn. My mother scrubbed floors to earn enough to feed us, and I remember her coming home at night so tired she could barely stand up—until finally the hard work killed her.'

He drew himself up, unaware that she had gone white as she heard what he said. He'd kept the memories inside him for so long and yet suddenly they came tumbling out, tainted by the pain he felt even now. 'My mother died when I was fourteen. It was breast cancer, which had gone untreated because she'd been too busy and too scared to seek help until it was too late.

'I know what the *real* world is like, you see. It was my world and there were no nannies or chauffeurs, no pony-club meetings. It was a world of going without and making do, and I promised myself that I would escape from it somehow. I did, and I make no apology for it. So don't you dare stand there and tell me how I should feel, because you don't have any idea what you're talking about!'

He walked out of the room, leaving her standing there. What she was thinking at that moment he had no idea and didn't care. Dorothy was in the corridor and it was clear from her expression that she'd heard what he'd said. She moved aside as Stephen went into the office and he was glad that she didn't say anything.

He didn't want to hear anything right then, didn't want to listen to any words of comfort or reproach. It had been years since he'd let loose the memories of those days and now he wasn't sure he could handle them. If there was one thing he regretted more than anything, it was that his mother hadn't lived long enough to see him escape from the trap of poverty.

'I'm sorry. I had no right... I didn't know, Stephen!'

He couldn't ignore the anguish in her voice, even though it took all his will-power to turn and face her. She was standing in the doorway, and even from that distance he could see the glitter of tears in her eyes. It shocked him to see them. Why was she crying? Who was she crying for? For herself because his angry words had upset her? Or for him because what he had told her had touched her?

It was that last thought which melted the remains of his anger. 'It's OK,' he said quietly. 'How could you have known?' He gave her a crooked grin, shaken by how good it felt to know that she cared. Alex *cared* that he was hurting and that helped ease the pain more than he would have thought possible. 'It isn't something I usually go around talking about.'

She managed a wobbly smile but it didn't conceal the regret in her beautiful green eyes. 'I guessed that. But I am sorry, Stephen. Truly. I had no right to say what I did and I apologise for it.'

He shrugged, wanting suddenly to lighten the mood. His emotions were already raw so that it was hard to get the right balance. Obviously, she cared that she had hurt him but he shouldn't go reading too much into it. 'Apology accepted. Let's forget about it—'

He stopped abruptly as the sound of a sudden squeal of air brakes, followed by an almighty crash that made the whole building shake, carried clearly into the room. 'What the devil was that?'

He was out of the room at a run, with Alex hard on his heels. He raced out of the front door and down the drive, his heart turning over as he took in the scene of chaos that met them. A tanker had overturned at the corner of the road. There were several other cars involved as well and a few pedestrians lying on the pavement.

'Heaven help us!' Dorothy had followed them outside and she pressed a hand to her mouth as she saw what had happened. Stephen gave her arm a gentle squeeze as he saw how shaken she was. 'Can you ring for the emergency services, Dorothy? Explain that they'll need to send ambulances and a fire engine.'

He looked at Alex as the elderly receptionist hurried off. 'We'd better get down there and see what we can do.'

She didn't waste time answering as she swiftly followed him down the road. Several passers-by had stopped to help and had already lifted a couple out of one of the cars. Stephen sent up a quick prayer that neither of them had suffered spinal injuries as he turned to Alex.

'I'm going to check on those people they've got out. Can you make sure that nobody else is moved until we're certain it's safe to do so?' he ordered tersely.

Alex nodded, her face reflecting his own concern. 'The last thing we want is someone with a fractured spine being moved.'

'Exactly.' He gave her a grim smile then hurried over to the couple from the car. They were badly shaken but, apart from a few cuts and bruises, seemed otherwise unhurt. Leaving them in the care of a group of bystanders, he crossed the road to where a small crowd was clustered around a woman lying on the pavement.

'I'm a doctor. Can you let me through, please?' He knelt down beside the woman as people moved aside, his heart turning over as he saw that it was Debbie Francis, Danny's mother. She was deeply unconscious and her pulse was weak and far too rapid when he checked it.

Stephen made himself focus on what injuries she had sustained, knowing that he couldn't allow any personal feelings to get in the way. Thoughts of how Danny was going to cope with his mother injured had to wait till later.

He systematically began to check her over and saw straight away that she had an open fracture of the right tibia. The bone was protruding through the flesh and he realised that he needed his bag so that he could cover the wound and prevent any infection getting in. He looked round at the group of onlookers and was relieved when he spotted a familiar face.

'Mrs Murphy, can I ask you to go to the surgery and get my case? Dorothy is there and she'll give it to you,' he said.

'Of course. I'll be as quick as I can, Dr Spencer.'

Mrs Murphy bustled off, obviously delighted to have been singled out for such an important job. Stephen carried on with his examination, running his hand delicately over Debbie's skull and frowning when he found a massive lump on the back of her head. Mrs Murphy arrived back with his bag at that moment so he quickly found the torch and raised Debbie's lids to shine it into her eyes, frowning in concern as he saw how her pupils dilated unevenly.

'How is she?' Alex came and knelt beside him, her face mirroring his concern as she saw what was happening. 'Possible brain injury?' she said quietly so nobody could overhear.

'Looks like it.' Stephen's tone was grim as he put the torch away then set about covering the wound on Debbie's leg. 'How's it looking over there? Is everything sorted out now?'

'Yes. Luckily there was an off-duty policeman passing, and he's taken charge. Most of the car passengers are OK, a bit shaken up but otherwise unhurt. They're being taken to the school hall for now.' Alex glanced along the road and frowned. 'It's the driver of the tanker who's the main problem now. He's trapped in his cab.'

'How bad is he?' he asked, as he finished taping the dressing into place.

Alex shook her head. 'I've no idea. The policeman wouldn't let me go too near until he'd checked out what was being carried in the tanker. Evidently, some of the load has spilled out onto the carriageway and he isn't sure how hazardous it is.'

'Just what we need!' Stephen groaned. He glanced up as someone arrived with a blanket. He draped it over Debbie then stood up and looked around. Traffic was at a standstill and the whole road was now blocked with vehicles. Several people had got out of their cars to see what was going on, adding to the confusion.

He frowned as he checked his watch. 'How long is that ambulance going to be? She needs to be transferred to hospital immediately.'

'Dorothy said to tell you that there's a traffic jam in the centre of town. They're having trouble getting through, with it being rush-hour,' Alex explained, sounding as concerned as he was by the news.

'That means the fire brigade will probably be delayed as well. And then they're going to have to get through this lot. Damn!' Stephen sighed heavily as he realised it was going to be some time before help arrived. He quickly made up his mind.

'We need to take a look at the tanker driver. We can't just wait till the ambulance gets here. Can you see if that policeman has had the all-clear yet on that spillage? I'll organise someone to keep a watch on Debbie and let us know if there's any change in her condition, although I'm afraid there's little more we can do for her here.'

'I'll go and check.' Alex hurried away. She wasn't gone long and in the meantime Stephen enlisted Ellen Murphy's help once more. She seemed a sensible sort of woman and listened carefully as he explained what she must watch out for.

'Leave it to me, Doctor. I'll keep an eye on her, to be sure.'

'Thanks.' He smiled his gratitude then went to meet Alex as he saw her hurrying back across the street. 'Well?'

'Apparently the tanker is carrying some sort of oil used in cattle feed. It isn't toxic but it could be flammable if it comes into contact with a naked flame,' she explained.

'Then the biggest danger is if the engine catches fire,' he said thoughtfully. 'So far it doesn't look as though that's going to happen, but it's always a risk.'

'But we can't leave the driver there much longer, without seeing how badly hurt he is,' she protested.

He smiled at her vehemence. 'No, we can't. So shall we see what we can do, Dr Campbell?'

'You took the words right out of my mouth, Dr Spencer,' she replied.

Maybe it was the seriousness of the situation that prompted the levity but Stephen knew that it felt good to be so much in accord with Alex for once. He led the way to the tanker, stopping *en route* to tell the policeman what they intended to do. He immediately offered his help, which Stephen gratefully accepted.

The tanker was lying almost completely on its side. The roof of the cab had become wedged against a wall which had stopped it rolling completely over. Stephen climbed carefully onto the passenger door and peered through the side window. The driver was slumped sideways in his seat and appeared to be unconscious. It was impossible to tell how badly injured he was until they examined him, but Stephen wasn't happy with his colour.

'I don't like the look of him at all,' he told the others as he jumped down off the cab. 'He's unconscious and extremely pale. Let's see if we can get this door open and take a look.'

It was easier said than done because either the force of the accident had jammed it shut or it was locked from the inside. It defied all their attempts to open it.

'This isn't achieving anything.' Alex voiced all their thoughts as she stood panting from her exertions. She shot an assessing look at the vehicle and frowned. 'The driver's window is open. Maybe I can crawl between the gap in the wall and the cab and get in through there. I'll be able to open the door from the inside if it's locked.'

'It's too risky,' Stephen vetoed firmly. 'There's no way of knowing how stable the vehicle is for starters. If that wall gives way you could be pinned underneath it. We'll have to find another way.'

He looked around for an alternative then felt his heart leap into his throat as from the corner of his eye he saw her hurrying round the back of the tanker. 'Don't! Stay where you are.'

She gave no sign that she'd heard him as she disappeared into the narrow space between the vehicle and the wall. Stephen exchanged a worried glance with the policeman, silently endorsing his muttered sentiment about 'bloody women'. He had never felt so helpless or so scared as he ran to the front of the cab and watched her wriggling first her head and shoulders and then the rest of her body through the window.

The seconds seemed to be the longest he'd ever experienced before he heard her give a small triumphant cry. 'It was locked! Try it now,' she instructed from inside the cab.

Stephen was first to climb up on the side of the cab to try the door. The relief he felt when it suddenly opened was so great that his legs seemed to turn to water. It took every scrap of control he possessed not to let the others know how he felt, but there was a note in his voice which must have hinted at it because he saw Alex's eyes darken as he said tersely, 'Right, let's see what we've got, shall we?'

She didn't say anything, however, simply wedged herself in the passenger-side footwell and checked the man's pulse. 'Pulse rapid and rather weak. Breathing is very laboured as well.' She glanced over her shoulder to where Stephen was kneeling on the edge of the seat. 'Chest injury?'

'More than likely. He was probably thrown forward as well as sideways with the impact. He could have hit the steering-wheel. We need to get a neck brace on him before we move him, though. There should be one in my bag.'

The police officer hurried off to fetch it while he and Alex checked for any other signs of major injury. The driver started to come round while they were doing so, groaning in pain as he attempted to sit up.

'What happened?' he asked dizzily.

'Stay still!' Stephen instructed, worried about the damage he could do to himself. 'You've been involved in an accident. The tanker has rolled onto its side, but the fire brigade is on its way and they'll soon have you out. Oh, thanks.'

He took the neck brace from the policeman and passed it to Alex. 'You'll have to put this on. I can't reach.'

'No problem.' Quickly and deftly she fastened it around the driver's neck, ignoring his protests. She had just finished when he gave a gasp of pain and clutched his chest.

'It…feels…as…though…there's…a…knife…sticking in… me…' he gasped between increasingly laboured breaths.

Stephen frowned as he glanced at Alex. 'Sounds as though a broken rib could have pierced the chest wall.'

'I'll take a look.' She quickly unfastened the man's check shirt. 'Yes. You're right. I can see it.' She looked worriedly at the driver, who had his eyes closed now as he struggled for breath. 'Definite signs of cyanosis, Stephen. His left lung has obviously collapsed.'

'And the more air that gets sucked into the thorax through

that open wound the worse it will get. The other lung will stop working soon if we're not careful,' he added grimly, turning to the policeman again. 'We need a piece of clean plastic, something that won't allow any air to get through. Can you see what you can find?'

The officer nodded, wasting no time on questions as he hurried off. Stephen turned to Alex once more. 'Keep your hand over the wound to stop the air being sucked through it. I'm going to make a pad out of some sterile dressings. We'll fix that over the wound then cover it with the plastic and tape it down to make a temporary seal. It should do the job until the ambulance gets here.'

She nodded her understanding, gently placing her hand over the wound on the driver's chest. There was a slight improvement in his breathing but not very much. Stephen quickly fashioned a pad out of some dressings and passed it to her just as the officer arrived back with a piece of bright yellow plastic, gaily printed with luminous red poppies.

'Old lady over there wants to know if this will do. Apparently it's her rain hood,' he explained, offering it to Stephen for his inspection.

Stephen grinned. 'Let's just hope that we don't have a downpour!'

The officer laughed then helped Stephen by holding the triangle of plastic while he cut it into shape. Stephen passed it to Alex, cutting strips of adhesive tape for her to stick it down with and handing them to her one at a time. It wasn't the easiest of jobs, working in the confined space of the cab, but she seemed to manage extremely well. But, then, she wasn't the sort of person who would make a fuss, he thought. She would just get on with the job, without complaining. His admiration for her increased as he realised it.

By the time the emergency services finally arrived things were more or less under control. Stephen had sent Alex off to stay with Debbie, using the excuse that the young woman needed monitoring to get his colleague away from the tanker. The vehicle felt increasingly unstable and he was worried that the wall could give way any moment under its weight. It was a relief when the fire brigade arrived and quickly fitted air bags underneath to take the strain off the wall.

It was a long, tedious process, made even more difficult by the oil leaking from the tank. The police cordoned off the area, putting a total ban on anyone smoking while the fire brigade worked. Stephen and the paramedics supervised matters as the driver was finally freed from his cab. He was rushed straight off to hospital.

'Are you all right?' Alex came to join him as he walked back up the road.

'Just about. How about you?' he asked, running a hand tiredly round the back of his neck.

'OK, I think.' She sighed as they walked back to the surgery together. 'I hope Debbie is going to be all right. She still hadn't come round when they took her away in the ambulance.'

'All we can do is keep our fingers crossed,' Stephen said sadly.

'And pray,' Alex added softly.

He smiled at her. 'Maybe that's the most important thing of all.'

Dorothy was waiting for them when they got back. She had the kettle on and as soon as she saw them made them both a cup of tea. 'Here you are, drink this up. You look as though you both need it!'

'You're a mind-reader.' Stephen kissed her cheek, smiling as she gave him a little push.

'Get on with you!' She sobered suddenly. 'Ellen Murphy said as it was young Debbie who was hurt. How is she?'

'Not too good, Dorothy,' Alex said quietly, sipping her tea.

'Oh, you just never know what's going to happen, do you?' The receptionist sighed. 'It's that little lad of hers I feel sorry for. What's he going to do with his mum in hospital?'

'I've no idea. Debbie told me that she doesn't have any family who could help out,' Stephen said worriedly, putting down his cup. 'I wonder if young Danny knows what's happened?'

Alex frowned. 'I doubt it. He wasn't with Debbie so he must be at home. What do you think we should do, Stephen? We can't just leave him there on his own.'

'I'm going round there to make sure he's all right,' he informed her, heading for the door. He paused as a sudden thought struck him. 'What about surgery, though?'

'Leave me to worry about that,' she said swiftly. She gave him a smile which was full of understanding. 'You go and sort Danny out. I'll hold the fort here.'

'Thanks.' He didn't say anything else before he hurried upstairs to get his car keys but he didn't need to, he realised. Alex understood how important it was to him to make sure the boy was looked after. Maybe she had realised it before he had, in fact, and he felt slightly bemused by the thought.

How had she understood that in an odd way he saw himself in the child because Danny's situation mirrored his own childhood experiences? It hadn't occurred to him before that that was why he was so interested in the boy's welfare, but now he understood. Funny that Alex should have seen that so quickly, he mused, but she was nothing if not perceptive.

Bearing in mind what she'd said only that morning about him being happy with the life he had created for himself, that thought was somewhat unsettling. He sighed as he got into his car. One way or another, Alex Campbell had a rare ability to put her finger on the pulse of what made him tick, even though he had difficulty returning the compliment!

'So, would you like me to take you to hospital to see your mum?' Stephen asked quietly. He had gone straight to the flats and had spent a worrying five minutes when he hadn't been able to get any reply from the Francises' flat. It was sheer luck

that he'd happened to knock next door and had discovered that
Darla was keeping an eye on Danny.

He'd quickly explained what had happened to her then had
gone in and told the boy about the accident, doing his best to
keep things as low key as possible so as not to frighten him.
However, it was obvious from the child's quivering lips that
he was scared stiff.

'Mum isn't going to…die, is she?' the boy muttered, wiping
his nose on the sleeve of his jumper.

Stephen passed him a tissue from the box Darla offered him,
smiling at the girl's thoughtfulness. 'Thanks. Your mum is very
poorly, Danny, but the doctors and nurses are going to do all
they can to make her better.'

'Look how they made my mum well again,' Darla put in,
getting up to give the little boy a hug. 'Debbie will be fine,
you'll see!'

She glanced at Stephen for confirmation and he managed to
summon up a few words of encouragement, wishing he could
be as confident. Debbie had been very badly injured and it
would take her some time to recover…if she did recover, that
was.

He chased away that thought as Danny suddenly nodded. 'I
want to go and see her.'

'Then I'll take you there. How about if you show Darla
where your mum keeps her nighties and things so that she can
help you pack a bag?' he suggested.

'OK.' Danny looked a bit brighter at being given something
to do. Darla went with him while Stephen put a call through
to the hospital to see if there was any news on Debbie's condition. He was told that she was in the operating theatre and
that there was no news as yet.

He sighed as he went to meet the two youngsters. With a
bit of luck there would be some news by the time he got Danny
to the hospital, and he could only hope that it would be good
news. After that he would have to decide what to do with the

little boy. He couldn't bring him back here to the flat and leave him by himself, neither could he expect Darla to look after him. The only other option, that of contacting Social Services, was one he shied away from until he knew what Debbie would want to do. Which meant that for the time being he would have to take charge of Danny himself.

Stephen smiled ruefully. He hadn't realised the half of what this job would entail when he'd agreed to help Graham out!

CHAPTER SEVEN

'IT'S all arranged. Rita is coming round here for Danny. Evidently, he knows her quite well because she helps out at his school three mornings a week. Dorothy suggested it and Rita agreed immediately, bless her. He's going to stay with them until Debbie is out of hospital.'

Alex had come to tell Stephen about the arrangements, slipping into his room between appointments. It was another busy morning but the patients were too busy discussing the accident to grumble about the wait they were having.

'That's great!' Stephen sat back in his chair with a sigh of relief. 'Will you tell Rita that I'll collect him around three this afternoon so that we can pop back to the hospital to see his mother?'

'Will do. Is there any news about Debbie and the driver yet?' she asked.

'Both of them came through their operations all right. Debbie has had the blood clot removed from her brain and the surgeon is fairly confident that she'll be fine once she regains consciousness. As for the driver, the consensus is that he was extremely lucky.' Stephen frowned as he thought back to those frightening minutes when Alex had crept into the cab. 'If you hadn't put yourself at risk like that he might not have made it.'

'All part of the job, isn't it?' She dismissed his praise with a quick smile then hurried from the room. Stephen picked up the notes for his next patient, still frowning. All part of the job, she'd said, but this job entailed so much more than he'd anticipated. Oh, he enjoyed working at his own practice but he rarely got as involved with the patients as he was doing here.

It added a different dimension to the work, a new responsibility. It made him see that what he did could and would make a difference to people's lives. The idea both appealed to and worried him.

How could he be sure of doing the right thing and making decisions that would improve things for them?

The simple answer was that he couldn't be sure. All he could do was his best. As long as he cared enough, things should work out...

He felt a jolt of surprise as the thought settled. He *did* care, although he'd never thought he would. He'd believed that he'd walk away after the six weeks were up and that would have been that. However, he knew it was going to be harder than he'd imagined.

It would be a wrench to leave when the time came, he admitted. That it would be an even bigger wrench to leave one particular person was something he didn't want to think about. The thought of walking away from Alex when the time came was deeply...unsettling?

Stephen sank back onto the sofa and closed his eyes. It was eight p.m. and he had just completed twelve hours of solid work. His whole body was aching with tiredness yet he felt a deep sense of satisfaction as well that he'd achieved so much.

Lifting the glass to his lips, he took a sip of the wine he'd poured for himself, still keeping his eyes closed. He'd put a record on Graham's less-than-state-of-the-art stereo and it provided a soothing background. He was hovering on the brink of sleep when the door suddenly opened.

'Oh, sorry. I didn't realise that you were—'

'Catnapping?' He opened his eyes and grinned at Alex, who was standing uncertainly in the doorway. 'I'll admit to that but not to the fact that I was almost asleep!'

'The pressure getting to you, is it?' she teased as she came into the room. She went to the table by the window and picked up a paperback novel. 'No wonder after the day we've had. Still, I won't disturb you. I only came for this.'

She held up the book, pausing when Stephen held out his hand. She gave it to him, waiting while he glanced at the picture on its cover then skimmed through the blurb on the back of the jacket. His brows rose as he gave it back to her.

'Hmm, I'd never have guessed you were a closet romantic, Dr Campbell.'

She laughed, not taking offence because she evidently sensed that none had been intended. 'We all have our little vices! I devour umpteen of these romance novels each week. I find them relaxing.' She folded her arms and gave him a considering look. 'So, come on, confess—what's your vice, Stephen?'

He smiled, as she'd intended him to, thinking how attractive she looked, standing there. She had changed out of her working clothes into khaki-green trousers which had a slight military flavour to their cut and colour. A plain white T- shirt left loose and bare feet completed the outfit. She looked very young and lovely in the casual outfit and Stephen wouldn't have changed a thing except maybe to free her hair from that far too tidy knot—

He caught himself up short, putting a block on the fantasies his traitorous mind was spinning. 'Who says that I have any?'

'Me for starters!' she retorted. 'You don't get to your age without succumbing to temptation at some point along the way.'

He clutched a hand to his heart and pretended he was in pain. 'Oh, you know where to hit a guy where it hurts most! My age? I'll have you know that I'm not a day over—'

'Thirty-five,' she put in smoothly. She raised her brows at his unconcealed astonishment. 'If you're wondering how I know that, guess.'

'Graham?' he suggested ruefully after only a minimum of hesitation.

'Spot on.' She sighed reflectively. 'I wonder if you realise just how often Graham talks about you?'

He picked up the wine bottle, suddenly uncomfortable with the idea of what his old friend might have said. 'I don't think I want to know the answer to that. How about a glass of wine while you're here? I'm only allowing myself this one glass as I'm on call tonight, so you'd be doing me a favour by drinking some of it.'

'Well…' She hesitated only a moment before she shrugged and sat down in a chair. 'Why not? Thanks.'

Stephen poured her a glass then set it down on the table beside her and picked up his own glass. 'How about a toast?'

'What to?' She sounded so wary that he chuckled.

'Are you always this cagey?' he teased, and earned himself a grudging laugh.

'Always!' she stated emphatically. 'I like to be one of the angels.'

'Fearing to tread, unlike the fool who rushes in?' He'd caught her drift immediately and saw the glimmer of surprise which lit her eyes before she raised the glass to sniff the wine's bouquet. He gave a deeply satisfied laugh, not bothering to hide his delight at having hit the mark so perfectly. 'Mmm, you certainly fit the part of an angel, Alex, but surely there are some occasions when you let your heart rule your head?'

'Oh, certainly. Who doesn't?' She quickly changed the subject. 'So what's the toast, then? This wine smells delicious so don't make me wait much longer to taste it!'

He smiled, letting her know that he understood she was simply avoiding the subject. He had already sensed what a private person she was so it was no surprise, although he had to admit that he would love to get her to open up a bit more about herself. Still, maybe patience would earn its own reward so he didn't push her.

'To overcoming all the difficulties the day has brought. Will you drink to that?' he said lightly, raising his glass.

'I shall indeed!' She chinked her glass to his then took a swallow of the wine and let it roll around her tongue appreciatively. 'This is delicious! It's obviously not one of the bottles Graham keeps at the back of the cupboard in case he's forced to invite anyone round for a meal!'

Stephen laughed softly. 'For a man who cares so much about other people, Graham is *extremely* unsociable, isn't he?' He sighed as he sipped his wine. 'I think the reason is that he doesn't take time for himself. He's so busy caring for others that he sees it as a waste of time to indulge himself in any way.'

'You're right, of course. I've been here six months and in that time I can't recall him ever having a day off to do something *he* wants to do.' She drew her legs up under her, frowning as she held the ruby red wine to the lamp and studied the richness of its colour. 'He makes me feel guilty sometimes just by his sheer dedication to the job.'

'He would hate it if he knew that,' Stephen observed quietly. 'All Graham ever wants is that people live their lives as they want to live them. If they can help someone else along the way, that's fine. But he doesn't expect anyone to try to live by his standards. That's what makes him so special.'

She laughed softly. 'You two could form your own mutual admiration society. You talk about Graham in the same way he talks about you.'

Stephen grimaced to hide his embarrassment. 'Sorry.' He got up to change the record on the stereo as it came to an end, glancing quizzically at her over his shoulder. 'Country-and-western or jazz? What's your preference?'

'Oh, country-and-western without a doubt.' She laughed melodically, settling back in the chair as she sipped her wine. 'I already admitted to being a romantic at heart, didn't I?'

Stephen rolled his eyes as he slid the old vinyl disc onto the turntable. 'You call being thrown in jail or travelling the railroads romantic?' He shook his head as he went and sat down again. 'What a sad case you are, Alexandra Campbell!'

'Cheek! And country-and-western music isn't all jail and railroads, I'll have you know,' she retorted pithily.

He twirled the wine in his glass, watching her over its rim. There was a gentle flush on her cheek-bones now, a softness to her expression he didn't recall having seen before. Both served to make her look even more beautiful and desirable. 'So you're a stand-by-your-man sort of woman, are you?' he said, only half teasing.

'If and when I ever find the man I want to stand by then yes. Fidelity is the most important part of a relationship to my mind. Once I find the man I want to marry I shall stand by him through thick and thin,' she affirmed quietly.

'That's a rare view in today's world. Most people seem to view relationships as disposable. If they don't work out so what? There's always a new one further along the road.'

'But you don't feel that way do you, Stephen?' Her tone was gentle as she asked the question and he wondered if that was why it sounded more like a statement than anything else. She gave a faintly self-conscious laugh when he frowned. 'Sorry. None of my business.'

'Why not? I've just asked you how you feel so you're entitled to ask me the same question.' He paused, letting his thoughts gel into some sort of cohesive order, realising with surprise that he'd never considered it before. 'Yes, you're right. It isn't my view. When I marry it will be for ever. If there are difficulties I'll make sure we work through them.'

He shrugged. 'I can't see any point in making the commitment in the first place if you're not going to stick with it.'

Alex reached for the wine bottle and topped up her glass. She took a drink, before replying. 'I agree with you. I grew up in a household where promises were made only to be broken and where marriage was worth nothing more than the scrap of paper which made it legal.'

'It must have been hard.' Deliberately, he kept his tone light, sensing that she wanted to talk and yet afraid that he might scare her off by showing too much interest.

'It was…uncomfortable, shall I say? There was always an atmosphere, you see, a sort of undercurrent which I sensed even as a child. My parents always seemed to be trying to score points off one another. Could my mother have more affairs than my father? Could he find younger and younger girlfriends?

'I used to wish that we could be an ordinary family, living in an ordinary house—like those houses you see in commercials for washing-up liquid or fish fingers or something.' She laughed self-consciously. 'You must think I'm mad. Fish fingers, indeed!'

'It could have been stock cubes—then I'd really think you'd lost it!' he teased, before sobering abruptly. 'And, no, I don't think you're mad because I understand exactly what you mean. I used to feel that way, too. Oh, I know my situation was different to yours, but I used to wish that we were a *real* family, with a father who came home at night and a mother who didn't have to work all hours and was there when I got home from school to ask how my day had been.

'I suppose that's why it's important to me that if and when I ever marry it will be for good. I want my children to have the security I never had.'

'It must have been awful for you when your mother died,' Alex said softly. She shrugged when he glanced at her. 'At least I had a certain stability because there were always people around to take care of me, even if they were being paid to do so. But you had nobody, did you, Stephen?'

'No.' He sighed as he rested his head against the back of the seat and closed his eyes. 'I was absolutely devastated when it happened. I don't think I could really take it in at first. Then it was as though all the grief I felt turned to anger.'

He paused as the memory of those days came rushing back. Maybe he had unlocked the floodgates that morning but suddenly it was all there in his head, everything he'd felt after his mother's death.

His voice grated as he continued but he was speaking more to himself now, exorcising ghosts which probably should have been exorcised many years before. 'I think I went a bit crazy. I got in with a bad crowd and things might have got worse if it hadn't been for Graham.'

He tossed back the rest of his wine and set the glass on the table. Alex was watching him, her green eyes shadowed as she absorbed what he was telling her. He felt a momentary qualm at what he was revealing but the memories wouldn't be held back any longer. He had to tell someone! And who better than her? She would understand. Suddenly, through all the confusion of thoughts that one was so clear and sharp that his breath caught—Alex would understand.

'What happened, Stephen? Tell me.'

He smiled, letting his eyes rest on her beautiful face, drawing courage from just looking at her. 'I blamed the doctors for not being able to save my mother, you see. I had no idea how ill she had been, or that she should have sought help sooner. It was a simple gut reaction because I needed someone to blame. So one night I came here to the surgery because I wanted to teach one of them a lesson. Graham's car was in the drive. I'd picked up a stick which was lying on the ground and I was just about to set about it when he came out of the house.'

He ran his hand through his hair, aware that it was trembling. 'He asked me what I was doing and when I told him he said to carry on. If it made me feel better then do it, take my anger out on the car, but he knew of a better way if I was man enough to consider it.'

He laughed hoarsely, recalling those few minutes which had changed his life. 'The thing that struck me most was that he didn't give a damn about his car. All he was worried about was making *me* feel better!'

'That's typical of Graham,' she said huskily, then buried her face in her glass. Stephen frowned because he could have sworn she was crying, but it was impossible to be sure. He hesitated but the urge to unburden the whole sorry story was simply too great.

'It is. Anyway, I was intrigued enough to come inside the house and listen to what he had to say. In a nutshell, it was that I could get even with the disease which had killed my mother by learning how to fight it and how to fight other diseases that killed other people. It just depended on whether I was man enough to accept the challenge.'

'And you were? That's why you became a doctor, isn't it, Stephen?' There was no mistaking that she was crying now, and he frowned as he saw the tears sliding down her cheeks.

'What's the matter?' he said, getting up to go over to her.

'Nothing.' She gulped as she ran her hand over her eyes and attempted to smile.

'Oh, Alex, sweetheart, don't!' He drew her to her feet, feeling guilty about upsetting her. 'I never meant...'

'I know you didn't!' She pressed her fingers against his mouth to stop the apology. Her eyes were as deep and green as the ocean as they skimmed his anguished face. 'I know that you weren't trying to...to play on my sympathy.'

He wanted to say something but that would have meant losing the contact between her fingertips and his mouth, and suddenly that idea was unbearable. Even now the gentle pressure was sending signals to each and every cell in his body, putting them on alert, warning them that something new, scary, marvellous, was happening...

He moved his head a fraction so that her fingertips slid across his mouth and felt the burst of sensation run down his body until it reached the soles of his feet. He wasn't aware of making any sound but knew he had as he saw her eyes widen, but oddly she didn't remove her hand. It was as though now she'd made the contact she, too, found it impossible to break it. His mouth was the magnet and her fingers were drawn to it, clinging…

He let the tip of his tongue slip between his lips and taste her skin, hearing the quick, sharp breath she took. Her own lips parted on a tiny sigh of pleasure or surprise so that they perfectly mirrored the shape of his. He could see the pink tip of her tongue mimicking his actions as he tasted her sweetly flavoured flesh once again, and almost moaned out loud.

How could anything so innocent be so erotic? he wondered giddily, but he already knew the answer. *Everything* about Alex was a stimulant to him!

Reaching up, he captured her hand, slowly and deliberately kissing each fingertip in turn before gently lowering it to her side. She made no sound, even though he knew that she understood what was going to happen next.

He gave her time to draw back if she wanted to and was filled with a fierce elation when she made no attempt to move. She knew that he was going to kiss her but it was what she wanted as much as he did!

Her mouth was so soft beneath his, soft and cool and addictive! As his lips settled over hers, Stephen suddenly knew that one kiss was never going to feed this hunger he felt. He went quite still, suddenly afraid that he was taking a step into the unknown. In his experience kisses were given and received without it being an earth-shattering event, but this was different. This kiss had the power to change his life and the thought scared him until he realised that already it was too late to do anything about it. The die had been cast with the very first taste of Alex's mouth…

She gave a small murmur of pleasure as his mouth settled more firmly over hers, her hand going up to cup the back of his head as though she were afraid that he might break away from her. No chance of that! he thought wryly before he lost the ability to think at all. There was just the drugging sweetness of her mouth and the way it clung to his, how her lips parted so readily and willingly so that his tongue could slip inside...

He almost keeled over as he felt the warm moistness of her tongue synchronising with the movement of his in the most seductive of dances. Rockets seemed to be going off inside his head, blinding flashes of colour flickering against his closed lids, a vapour trail of heat coursing through his limbs.

He drew her closer, needing to feel her body against him to ease the ache which was growing stronger with each second that passed. It worked for a few minutes, her softly feminine curves settling against his male hardness as though their bodies had been sculpted to fit together like two perfect halves of one whole. But soon the feel of her created its own ache, its own need, so that kissing her and holding her wasn't nearly enough.

He wanted to make love to her! His mind screamed out the thought, tempting him, tormenting him with images of how it would be to lie in bed with Alex beside him, beneath him, above him. If it had been anyone else maybe he would have given in. But this was Alex and this was too important to spoil by going too far or too fast too soon.

He slackened his hold on her, letting his lips skim up her cheek, leaving behind a trail of butterfly-soft kisses in their wake. He pressed a gentle kiss to her temple then slowly— because it took him such a lot of effort—made himself step back. There was a second when she just stood there, looking so bemused and beautiful that he nearly forgot all his good intentions. And then she took a deep breath and took a step of her own backwards, away from him.

'I...' She stopped and had a quick rethink, smoothing her face into a deliberately bland expression which no longer fooled him as it had. Beneath that frosty exterior there was a warm, live woman, a woman who was caring and compassionate, a woman who was determined and brave, a woman he could very easily fall in love with if it hadn't been too soon even to think about such a thing!

'I think I'll get an early night.' That was what she came up with and he hid a smile. That she was as shaken as he felt was beyond question but she was trying her best to pass it off like the woman she was.

'Of course. It's been a long day, Alex, hasn't it?' he offered blandly, and earned himself a sharp look.

'It has. It's been quite, well, traumatic one way and the other. It's no wonder…' She tailed off, obviously not sure which way to go about making the suggestion.

'That people act in a manner they might otherwise not have done?' he suggested with a pedantry that earned him another, even sharper look.

'Yes. Goodnight, Stephen. I'll see you in the morning…in surgery.'

Oh, nicely done, he thought as he watched her walk from the room with her head held high and her spine rigid. That should put him firmly back in his place. She was making sure he knew that the only role he had in her life was that of colleague.

He grinned wickedly as went to the rack of records next to the stereo. He was sure he'd spotted it… Yes!

He slipped it onto the turntable and cranked up the volume, then went to the door and opened it wide as the first plaintive chords filled the air. Leaning against the doorjamb, he listened while the singer sang her heart out, exhorting every woman to stand by her man…

A bedroom door slammed with enough force to make the house shake. Stephen grinned as he went and turned the music down a decibel or two. Message given and received. Now he would have to see how effective it had been…but that depended on how effective he wanted it to be, of course.

He frowned as he sat down again. Did he want Alex to think of him as *her* man? Was that what he would choose if a passing genie could have granted him one wish?

It gave him hot and cold chills just to think about it. By the time the record came to an end he still hadn't made up his mind. But some day soon he would have to decide and do something about it. The only fly in the ointment was that it could be an uphill struggle, convincing Alex that it was what *she* wanted if his decision was yes!

CHAPTER EIGHT

THE days flew by so that a week or more had passed before Stephen knew it. Life had settled down into some sort of routine and he found that he was enjoying the job more and more.

As to the situation between him and Alex, that seemed to have been put on a back burner. She had made no mention of him kissing her and Stephen hadn't brought the subject up. Frankly, he, too, preferred to forget about it because thinking about it only made life seem far too complicated! It was easier to let things lie even though he knew that he couldn't go on taking that approach for ever.

He had just finished surgery on Tuesday morning and was clearing his desk when Alex came to find him.

'You've not forgotten that you're taking the baby clinic this afternoon, have you?' she asked, coming into the room.

'No, I haven't,' he replied, taking care to keep his tone as even as hers had been as he glanced up. He felt his heart perform its customary somersault as he looked at her, trim and elegant in her navy suit. He quickly averted his face in case his expression gave him away. He might prefer to let things lie for now but that didn't mean he could ignore the effect she had on him.

'Is there anything I need to know beforehand?' he asked in a voice which was just a shade too flat.

'Not really. Sandra will be there so she'll be able to fill you in if there's a problem,' she replied levelly. 'She used to be the practice nurse here until she had to resign for family reasons. Now she just helps out on clinic days to keep her hand in, so to speak. It should be perfectly straightforward... Oh, there are half a dozen babies coming for hearing tests, which could be fun.'

Stephen grinned at the wry note in her voice. 'Chaos reigns supreme, eh?'

'Something like that!' She returned his smile, her green eyes resting on him for a few seconds longer than was strictly necessary so that his heartbeat quickened before she abruptly turned away. 'I'd better be off. I'll give Graham your regards when I see him, shall I?'

'Please. And tell him that I'll pop in tonight to see him. I promised Danny that I'd take him to see Debbie,' he explained as she glanced back in surprise. 'It will give Rita a break.'

'Dorothy told me that you've been paying for a taxi to take them to the hospital each day,' she said quietly. Her expression was hard to read. 'That was kind of you.'

He shrugged, uncomfortable with the praise. 'It isn't easy for Rita to get on and off buses so it seemed simpler.'

'Maybe. But not many people would have thought about it, Stephen.' She didn't add anything before she left but he couldn't deny the pleasure he'd felt at seeing the approval on her face.

He sighed as he gathered up the papers. Right from the beginning it had mattered what Alex thought of him, although originally he had been more concerned about her opinion of him *professionally*. Now, after that kiss, he had to face the fact that he cared what she thought about him *personally* as well. It was a sobering thought for a man who had taken little account of other people's opinions in the past.

'That all seems to be fine. Jodie has gained two ounces since your last visit, which is excellent.' Stephen lifted the squirming baby out of the scales and handed her to her beaming young mother.

'Eats me out of house and home, she does!' Donna Fielding

laughed as she settled the tiny girl on her lap and began dressing her again.

Stephen grinned as he sat behind the desk to jot down a few notes about the baby's general health. 'Well, she's coming along fine, Donna. You're doing a great job with her.'

The young mother blushed. Like so many of the mums he had seen that afternoon, she was little more than a child herself—just seventeen, in fact. 'Thank you. I didn't know how I'd cope at first, but once I'd been to the classes I had a better idea what to do. They were brilliant!'

'Classes? Do you mean the antenatal classes at the hospital?' Stephen queried, putting down his pen.

'Oh, no! Not them.' Donna's tone was scathing. 'I only went the once and didn't go again. The way some of those other mums looked down their noses at you…like you had no right to be having a baby!' She picked Jodie up and cuddled her.

Stephen frowned, still wondering what the girl had been alluding to. He glanced round as Sandra explained.

'Dr Campbell instigated a programme at the local high school on baby care. It's been a huge success, hasn't it, Donna?'

'It was brilliant!' the teenager replied enthusiastically. 'Dr Campbell explained everything and never made you feel stupid, like a lot of adults do. She just made sure that we knew how to take care of our babies…you know, what to feed them and how to bath them, things like that.'

'It sounds like it was an excellent idea. Were there many of you on the course?' Stephen asked, wondering when Alex had found the time to fit in this extracurricular activity. She must have done it in her own time—that was all he could assume, because their hectic schedule didn't allow much leeway.

'Five to begin with but a few more who'd had their babies came along once they heard about it. Dr Campbell didn't mind. She said the more the merrier as far as she was concerned. It was really good because I learned all about when I should give Jodie solids and what to do if she was feeling poorly.'

Donna picked up the baby and prepared to leave. She paused, a sudden frown darkening her pretty face. 'Dr Campbell was all right the other night, wasn't she? I…I heard what happened in the car park.'

'She's fine, thank you, Donna, although it could have been a very nasty incident,' Stephen assured her, wondering how news of the incident had got round. He had told no one about it and he doubted whether Alex would have mentioned it either.

He shook his head as Donna left. 'I wonder how she heard about that?'

'About what?' Sandra asked immediately. She sighed when he finished telling her about the scare Alex had had. Sandra seemed to be in her mid-thirties, although the lines of strain around her mouth made her look older. 'I imagine Donna heard about it from Darren.'

'Darren Richardson?' he queried, and saw her grimace.

'Didn't take you long to get to know about him!' she replied tartly. She suddenly frowned. 'I wonder if it was him who tried to snatch Alex's case that night? I wouldn't put it past him. He's a really nasty piece of work. I don't know what Donna sees in him as she's a nice enough girl. Darren is Jodie's father,' she added for Stephen's benefit.

'Oh, I see. That explains it. Donna might have heard him speaking about the incident.' He sighed heavily. 'It's just a pity that Alex didn't get a good look at the two lads who attacked her then she might have been able to make a positive identification for the police.'

'It probably wouldn't have made much difference.' Sandra shook her head. 'No, Darren would have had a watertight alibi, you take it from me!'

She sounded so convinced that there seemed little point in pursuing the idea. However, Stephen stored it away for future reference. 'Right, then, let's see who we have next.' He picked up a card from the pile on his desk. 'It's Luke Cartwright for a hearing test.'

The afternoon was hectic after that. Stephen enjoyed doing the routine hearing tests which all babies had when they attended the clinic. They were only very basic and involved little more than standing behind the child and shaking a rattle or squeaking a rubber toy to check that there was nothing wrong with their hearing. All passed with flying colours, to the relief of their mothers, then Sandra tidied up and put on her coat, sighing as she headed for the door.

'Well, it's back home to see how things have been there,' she announced wryly.

'That sounds as though you're expecting the worst,' Stephen joked, and she grimaced.

'I am! I live with my mum, you see, and she's got Alzheimer's. That's why I had to give up my job here as I couldn't manage to work full time and look after her. I have a sitter who stays with her when I come to the clinic but some days she can be very, well, difficult.'

'It must be hard,' he sympathised.

'It certainly isn't easy. Most days it's like looking after a stranger, not Mum. She doesn't really know who I am or where she is. Still, you just have to get on with it, don't you?' Sandra smiled. 'It was nice meeting you, Stephen. I've heard so much about you that it was good to see you in the flesh at long last!'

'Don't!' Stephen grimaced. 'I go hot and cold when I imagine what Graham has been saying!'

'Nothing bad, I can assure you! Graham is very fond of you. I think he sees you as the son he never had. Right, I'll be off, then. Cheerio.'

Stephen sighed as the door closed. Why had he never realised how devoted to him Graham was? He should have done because Graham had been so supportive over the years. It made him wonder once again about the suggestion Alex had made, that Graham was hoping he would take the post as director of the new health centre.

He frowned. It was odd, but the idea didn't seem nearly as unpalatable as it had done. Was that because the thought of working with Alex was such a temptation? He wasn't sure, but it would be foolish to rush into making a decision based on a lot of physical attraction plus one kiss!

'I've bought some steak—do you fancy sharing it with me?' Stephen offered, praying that Alex wouldn't guess how much he wanted her answer to be yes.

He put the carrier bag on the kitchen table and started unpacking its contents. It had been sheer impulse which had made him stop off at the supermarket on his way back from dropping Danny at Rita's flat. He certainly hadn't been planning on cooking dinner for them, but as he'd driven past the shop the thought had skipped into his mind: buy something nice and cook Alex a delicious dinner and then… What? That was the sixty-four-thousand-dollar question, of course, and he still hadn't made up his mind about the answer!

'Well…' Her hesitation was obvious and he fixed a smile into place so that she wouldn't guess how disappointed he was if a tentative yes became a positive no.

'It's not a problem,' he assured her lightly, 'although I expect you've got something planned as you're not on call tonight.'

'Simon mentioned something about calling round later—but there was nothing definite arranged,' she added quickly.

Stephen peeled the cling film off a tray of baking potatoes and selected one. He took a fork out of the drawer and gave it several vicious stabs, before popping it into the microwave. What was going on between her and this Ross fellow? Several times now Simon Ross had 'just happened' to drop by under some pretext or other. Were he and Alex just good friends or— heaven forbid—an item?

His heart heaved at that thought and he had to turn away in case she saw how much it troubled him. Taking the bag of mixed salad out of the carrier, he tossed it onto the draining-board, keeping his back towards her as he continued the conversation. Maybe he should have minded his own business but he wanted to know just how the land lay where Simon Ross was concerned.

'Maybe he'll want to take you out somewhere to eat, then?'

'Simon? You have to be joking!' Her laughter was quick and spontaneous and had him turning round to see what had prompted it.

'Why is that so funny?' he asked, his brows peaking steeply over puzzled grey eyes.

'Obviously you don't know Simon, otherwise you wouldn't have suggested it.' She grinned as she rooted through the carrier bag, came up with a pound of cherry tomatoes and popped one into her mouth. Stephen was almost beside himself with impatience as she chewed and swallowed. She couldn't come out with a statement like that, without explaining it!

He couldn't wait any longer as she delved into the bag once again. 'That sounded very cryptic. You can't leave me in suspense so tell me what you meant.'

'About Simon?' She smiled again as she examined the small, plump tomato. 'Simon is a brilliant doctor but he has one flaw—he's pathologically mean!'

She chuckled as she saw his face. 'I'm not joking, Stephen. That man makes an art form out of saving every penny! I wouldn't mind but his family is very well off—his parents are friends of mine, you see, so that's how I know him.'

Stephen wasn't sure whether he was pleased or not by the revelation. Obviously, Alex found Ross's fiscal habits less than attractive but the fact that they shared a common background had to work in his favour. A little more probing was definitely called for, although he refused to acknowledge why it was so important that he found out all he could.

'Obviously, you don't find this little flaw in his character a complete drawback,' he observed casually, 'otherwise you'd tell him to get lost.'

'Oh, I'm used to Simon's funny ways! And he's a good friend and can be a lot of fun as long as it doesn't entail him spending money.' She shrugged. 'Anyway, everyone's entitled to his...or her...little quirks.'

Well, he'd wanted to know so it was his own fault if he wasn't happy with the answer. Alex must be extremely fond of this Ross fellow if she was able to overlook this aspect of his character. Stephen shrugged, determined not to let her guess how that thought stung when put into context. Alex hadn't seemed inclined to make any concessions where *he* was concerned, but obviously that didn't apply in this case!

'I guess so. It would be a dull world if we were all the same. So, do you want to share this steak or what?' he asked with feigned indifference.

'Well... Yes, go on. But only if you let me help.' She had barely got the words out of her mouth when the phone rang. Stephen grimaced as he headed for the door.

'I may have been a little over-optimistic,' he said ruefully. He hurried along the hall and answered the phone, listening patiently to the garbled message the caller gave him before finally managing to get a word in edgeways. 'I'm on my way, Mrs Grimshaw. I want you to try and stay calm because it won't help your husband if you get upset. I'll be there in ten minutes.'

He went back to the kitchen, 'Mrs Grimshaw, Corporation Street. Evidently, her husband has, and I quote, ''had a funny turn''. I said I'd be right there so I'm afraid dinner will have to wait.'

Alex shrugged. 'All part and parcel of the job, isn't it? I'll give Barry Jones a call and tell him to meet you at the corner, shall I?'

'I really don't think there's any need—' Stephen began, then saw her face. 'OK, if you really think it's necessary.'

'There's no point in taking him on as a driver if you don't make use of his services,' she said firmly. 'Stop trying to be so macho, Stephen!'

He laughed at that. 'Sorry! I assure you that wasn't my intention.'

He hurried upstairs to collect his jacket then stuck his head round the door when he'd come back down. 'See you later. If it isn't too late maybe we can still have that meal?'

She shrugged. 'Actually, I'm starving so I think I'll just make myself a sandwich. Shall I put this lot in the fridge until you get back?'

'Yes. Thanks.' He gave her a quick smile, trying not to let her see his disappointment. He sighed as he went out to his car. He could recall quite clearly a time when he'd wanted a whole lot more than to spend an hour with a woman, dawdling over a home-cooked meal. How things had changed!

'I'll phone for an ambulance, Mr Grimshaw.'

Stephen drew the elderly woman away from the armchair where her husband was sitting, and lowered his voice. 'Your husband needs to be admitted to hospital immediately, Mrs Grimshaw. He's suffered a heart attack and that's the best place for him.'

'Oh!' Edna Grimshaw pressed a trembling hand to her mouth. 'I thought it was the pork. Albert kept saying as he had this terrible pain in his chest, and I told him it was indigestion because he'd had second helpings of crackling.'

'You mustn't blame yourself. It's just one of those things,' Stephen said, comfortingly. He excused himself, slipping out of the house to go to the car. Barry Jones was listening to the stereo but he switched it off as soon as he saw Stephen. A well-built young man in his early twenties, he had been thrilled by the offer of the job and so far had proved himself to be very reliable.

Stephen bent down to the open window. 'Can you ring for an ambulance, Barry, please? Tell them it's a heart attack.'

'Will do, Doc.' Barry looked pleased to be given the extra responsibility and quickly set about making the call, leaving Stephen free to go back inside.

Edna came hurrying to meet him as soon as he set foot through the door. 'How am I going to let my daughter know what's happened? She dotes on her dad, she does, and she'll want to be with him.'

'Is she on the phone?' Stephen bit back a sigh as the old lady shook her head. Few of the patients were on the telephone simply because the cost was so high for their limited budgets. 'Whereabouts does she live? I'll see if I can get in touch with her.'

'Will you? Oh, that is kind. It's Eve House, number seven-fifteen.' Edna had brightened up considerably as she hurried back to her husband to tell him the good news. Stephen waited there until the ambulance had collected Albert then went back to his car.

'Can we stop off at Eve House on the way back, Barry? Mrs Grimshaw's daughter lives there and she wants her to know what's happened to her father.'

'Sure thing, Doc,' Barry agreed affably. It didn't take them long to make the detour, and the Grimshaws' daughter was very grateful that he had taken the trouble to let her know what had happened. They were back at the surgery within the hour.

Barry pulled up in the drive, glancing at the car which was parked there, a rather elderly Ford. 'Looks as though Dr Campbell's got visitors.'

'Uh-huh.' Stephen replied noncommittally as he recognised Simon Ross's car. His mouth compressed at the thought of him and Alex cosily ensconced in the sitting-room, although he refused to admit that he was at all jealous. If he had *reservations* it was purely because he thought Alex could have done a lot better for herself than someone who counted every penny!

It was a relief when the car phone suddenly rang as another call came in. Stephen told Barry where to take him then firmly closed his mind to what might be going on inside the house. It was none of his business with whom Alex chose to spend her evenings…although he wished that it was!

CHAPTER NINE

STEPHEN decided to go home the following Saturday. There were some things he needed and he also wanted to check on any post that had arrived. Alex was covering surgery that morning, which left him free to head straight off after breakfast, yet he found himself hanging about.

Maybe he could persuade her to come along for the drive? he mused. It would be nice to have some company.

Oh, yes! his conscience jeered. And that was the *only* reason he intended asking her. It had nothing to do with the fact that he had been like a cat on a hot tin roof since Tuesday night when he'd come back to find Ross's car in the drive?

His mouth tightened as he ran upstairs to fetch his jacket. He had the uncomfortable feeling that it came a little too close to the truth. He wasn't happy with the thought that he was hanging about like some…some jealous teenager!

He had to pass the waiting-room on his way out and he frowned as he saw the number of people there. He backtracked to the office to have a word with Dorothy and see what was going on.

'Alex has been called out to an emergency. She'd barely got started when the call came in,' Dorothy explained worriedly. 'We don't usually have this many on Saturdays, with it being urgent cases only, but a whole crowd has turned up today!'

'I'd better take over for her. Send the first one in whenever you're ready, Dorothy, would you?' he offered immediately, earning himself a look of gratitude.

'Oh, you are a love! I didn't want to be late home today. Rita and I want to go to the market this afternoon to see if we can get ourselves new frocks for Elsie Jones's birthday do.'

Dorothy laughed. 'Although I can't see us getting much chance to try things on, with young Danny around! Kids are never fond of shopping, especially if it isn't for them.'

Stephen paused in the doorway, feeling suddenly guilty that he had left Dorothy and Rita to take care of the boy. 'How about if I take Danny with me? I'm going home to my flat to pick up some things so he can come along for the drive. We could stop off by the river afterwards,' he added.

'Oh, I'm sure he'd be thrilled! And it would mean me and our Rita could have the afternoon to ourselves.' Dorothy sounded delighted. 'Elsie has insisted that she wants this party to be really special because you're going as her partner!'

'I am?' Stephen rolled his eyes. 'Good job you told me because I hadn't realised that. Sounds as though I'm going to have to make a special effort, as well as you ladies.'

'Nothing less than a dinner jacket from the sound of it,' Dorothy teased, before hurrying off to sort out another patient who'd arrived.

Stephen sighed as he went to his room. What had he let himself in for?

By the time Alex got back it was gone eleven and Stephen had whittled the numbers down to just two people still waiting to be seen. He saw one and she saw the other and that was it. She came into the office as he was filing some notes and he gave her a warm smile.

'How are you? Dorothy said that you'd been called out to an emergency.'

'I was. I was having a fit, thinking about everyone waiting back here, but I couldn't leave the patient. It was an attempted suicide,' she added sadly. 'The poor woman had locked herself in the bathroom and it took us ages to persuade her to open the door. She'd taken half a bottle of paracetamol.'

'Tough,' he observed sympathetically. 'Cases like that take it out of you. Oh, I know you can treat the symptoms, although paracetamol is such a deadly drug once it gets into the liver, but it's the underlying reason why anyone would want to end her life which is the hardest to deal with.'

'Exactly. I feel almost as wrung out as the poor woman's husband,' Alex agreed, glancing round as Dorothy came in.

Stephen frowned as he took the opportunity to study her. She did look tired, he decided. There was a weary slump to her shoulders and a downward curve to her beautiful mouth that morning. But was it any wonder that she should be feeling the strain? From what he'd learned, Alex had been shouldering the brunt of the work load for quite some time.

'Right, I'll be off now. What a morning!' Dorothy grimaced as she zipped up her emerald green jacket then turned to Stephen. 'What time will you pick Danny up?'

He checked his watch. 'Half an hour be OK with you?'

'Fine.'

'Are you taking Danny to see Debbie this afternoon?' Alex asked once Dorothy had left.

He shook his head. 'No, he's going tonight with Rita. I offered to take him with me this afternoon to give them a break. Apparently, they want to go shopping for new dresses for Elsie Jones's party, and I thought it would be easier if they didn't have to trail young Danny round.'

'Ah, the party, of course.' Alex grinned at his look of surprise. 'I believe you are guest of honour. Meg was there when I visited Graham last night and she told me all about it.'

'Don't! This is getting out of hand. Is there nobody around here who doesn't know about my invitation?' he demanded, only half joking, and she laughed.

'I doubt it! This may be far removed from a village but news still travels fast. Still, it was good of you to offer to have Danny this afternoon.'

'It's not a problem.' He dismissed the praise as he turned to leave then stopped and mentally took a deep breath, before plunging in. 'I don't suppose you'd like to come along as well?

We could make an afternoon of it, take Danny down to the river then have tea afterwards.'

'I'm on call,' she began, but Stephen cut in quickly to over-rule her objection. It was about time she had a break, he decided. She couldn't go on, running herself into the ground, like this or she'd make herself ill. That it would also be nice to have some time with her away from the surgery was by the by, of course.

'I can get the on-call service to cover for a few hours,' he offered, holding up his hand when she immediately started to object. 'I know what you're going to say—that Graham only uses them for dire emergencies. Well, this might not fall into that category but, frankly, Alex, from the look of you, you do need a break.'

He waited for her to come up with a list of reasons why it was a bad idea and was surprised when she sighed. 'I suppose I do. It hasn't been easy these past few weeks...' She broke off but not before Stephen felt suffused with guilt at not having realised how difficult the situation had become.

She gave him a quick, almost shy smile. 'Well, if you're sure it won't mess up your plans, I'd love to come. Thank you.'

'Great!' he declared, then turned away in case she realised how delighted he was. It's just an outing to the river, Stephen, he told himself firmly, but that didn't stop his heart from racing with anticipation.

'I'll just go and make the arrangements.' That was all he said, however, as he went to his room to put a call through to the locum service. He sat back in his chair after it was done, trying to get himself back on an even keel, but it wasn't easy. Why should the thought of spending a few hours with Alex make him feel as though he wanted to shout from the rooftops?

The answer was lurking deep in his mind but he refused to let it come to the surface. For now it was enough to look forward to the rest of the day—he would worry about the consequences later!

*   *   *

'Wow! This is brill!'

Danny's voice was filled with awe as he stared into the state-of-the-art fishtank which Stephen had had installed not long after moving into the flat. He found it soothing to sit and watch the brightly coloured fish swimming around after a busy day at work. He went over to join Danny and Alex, who were engrossed in watching the fishes' antics.

'I'm glad you like it. I love sitting here at night, watching them swimming around.'

'It must be very relaxing,' Alex observed, turning to smile at him so that the bouncy curls swirled around her shoulders. It was the first time he'd seen her with her hair down and he couldn't help thinking how lovely she was, with the cameo-like perfection of her features framed by the mass of red-gold curls.

She'd dressed as casually as he had for the outing, in jeans and a creamy wool sweater with her feet pushed into old leather loafers, and looked more relaxed than he'd ever seen her. It seemed to augur well for the day, although he didn't let himself think about what he hoped to achieve by it other than to give her a much-needed break.

'It is,' he replied lightly, confining his thoughts before they ran away with him. He turned to Danny as the child claimed his attention.

'What's this one, Dr Spencer? Here.' The boy pointed to a beautiful red fish with blue stripes down its sides.

'That's a cardinal tetra.' Stephen bent to take a closer look at the fish and unwittingly drew in a lungful of Alex's perfume. It was an effort to find just the right casually informative note when Danny demanded a run-down on every fish in the tank.

'How about those over there that keep swimming through that archway?' Alex touched him on the arm to draw his attention to where she was pointing, and Stephen only just managed not to groan out loud. This was becoming more than any red-blooded male should be forced to endure! How on earth was he expected to keep his mind on the question with Alex standing beside him, her perfume filling his nostrils and her hand resting on his arm?

'They're angelfish,' he replied a trifle hoarsely. He cleared his throat. 'They tend to be a bit shy and keep well away from the others. I suppose cautious is the best way to describe them.'

'That figures!' She gave the huskiest of laughs which made the hair all over his body stand on end. Her eyes were very green when he glanced at her, the glow from the illuminated tank playing over her face and highlighting its delicate beauty. 'They hate rushing in as well.'

He understood her meaning immediately and his heart lifted as he was reminded of the conversation they'd had about her tendency towards caution. That she trusted him enough to make a joke at her own expense filled him with a mixture of elation and tenderness because he sensed it was something she rarely did. It was an effort not to let her know how much it had affected him and he replied as lightly as he could.

'Shows how much sense they've got, I'd say.' He straightened as Danny turned to him once more.

'I think they're just brill! I can't wait to tell Mum about them. I wish I had a pet,' the boy stated wistfully. 'I'd love a dog but Mum says that it would cost too much to feed and that it wouldn't be fair to keep it in a flat where there's no garden for it to play in.'

The child gave them a quick grin, sounding suddenly older than his eight years as he added, 'Still, maybe one day, eh?'

Stephen had to swallow the lump in his throat. He put his hand on Danny's shoulder and turned him towards the door. 'You never know what will happen, do you? Right, are we all ready for a bit of fun?'

'Yes!' Danny whooped with delight as he raced to the front door and flung it open.

'It gets to you, doesn't it, Stephen?'

He paused to glance at Alex, colour edging his cheek-bones

as he saw the understanding on her face. How had she guessed what he'd been thinking? He had no idea but it gave him an odd buzz to realise how well she understood him.

'It does. I remember feeling just the same at Danny's age,' he admitted, realising that he would have denied it to anyone else. However, it was impossible to lie to Alex. 'I would have given anything for a dog to love and take for walks but we just couldn't afford to keep one.'

'That's why you're such a good doctor—because you can empathise with your patients. You understand the problems they face in their lives and how they affect them because you've experienced them at first hand.' She lifted her head and looked him squarely in the eyes. 'It would be a waste not to make use of such a talent, Stephen.'

She didn't add anything more as she went to join Danny. Stephen followed them to the lift, joining in the conversation as best he could, but his mind was only partly on what was being said.

Was it a waste to forge a life for himself away from the one he'd known as a child? Should he be utilising his experience more? A couple of weeks ago he would have dismissed the idea but that had been before he'd met Alex. She kept making him re-examine his motives and it wasn't comfortable to realise that he had doubts.

He sighed as the lift came to a stop. While he was being honest he may as well admit that it mattered that she might think less of him if he decided that he couldn't continue working in the practice once Graham was better. But did she want him to stay *just* because he was a good doctor? Or was there another reason? It was crazy that his future might hang on knowing the answer to that question!

'Is it all right if I have a go on the swings? I'll be careful!'

Stephen groaned as he flopped down onto the grass. A riotous game of football had left him worn out but it seemed to have had little effect on the boy. 'Where do you get your energy from, young man? I wish you'd give me some!' He grinned as Danny laughed. 'All right, then, but no acting the fool. We don't want any accidents.'

'Promise!' Danny headed off to the playground and was soon happily swinging away. Once Stephen was sure he was following orders and not going too high, he relaxed. Leaning against a handy tree-trunk, he closed his eyes, savouring the feeling of contentment that stemmed from doing nothing more taxing than enjoying himself.

'He's having a great time, isn't he?' Alex murmured sleepily from where she was curled up on the tartan rug Stephen had dug out from the boot of his car. She rolled onto her side, propping her head on her hand as she watched Danny swinging away. 'I don't suppose Debbie gets much chance to take him out so it's a treat for him, coming here.'

'It's a treat for me, too,' Stephen said wryly, opening his eyes and thinking how beautiful she looked, lying there all relaxed and sleepy. 'I can't remember the last time I came to the park to play football!'

She laughed as she rolled onto her back again and stared at the sky. 'Not the usual sort of sophisticated entertainment you go in for, Dr Spencer? What do you normally do in your spare time, then?'

'Oh, I run or play squash and tennis…things like that.'

'Sounds very energetic to me.' She grimaced as she plucked a long blade of grass. 'You must do something a bit less taxing?'

'Not really. Apart from the odd dinner party, my time is mostly taken up with work. How about you?' he asked, settling into a more comfortable position. The muted sounds of people enjoying a day out by the river floated on the warm air but didn't really disturb the peace and quiet. He watched as a family clambered into one of the rowing boats which were for hire, mother, father and two small children all enjoying themselves.

They pushed away from the bank and Stephen smiled as he saw the oars splashing clumsily before the father, who was rowing, found the right rhythm.

They moved out of his line of sight and he glanced at Alex again, his brows rising questioningly. 'Well?'

'Oh, I read, listen to music, go to the odd concert...nothing special,' she said dismissively, tossing the grass away. 'I haven't had a lot of time to spare recently so I haven't done all that much.'

He sighed heavily. 'It isn't right that you should work so hard, Alex. Graham shouldn't let you.'

'It was my choice. Graham couldn't keep on the way he was. Physically he hasn't been up to it. Anyway, I knew what the job would be like when I took it so I'm not complaining,' she added firmly.

'Why did you take it, though?' Stephen frowned as he looked at her. 'Why *this* job in this practice? You must have had other offers so why did you choose a post which most doctors would have avoided like the plague?'

'Because I thought I could make a difference. That was important to me.' She shrugged when he continued to look at her. 'I've always been very aware of how fortunate I've been to have had everything I could possibly want, materially at least.'

'So you saw this as a way to even the score?' He was aware of the faintly sceptical note in his voice and shrugged when she glanced at him. 'Are you sure that you aren't being overly sensitive, Alex? It isn't your fault that you were born into a wealthy family. You shouldn't think that you have some sort of debt to repay to society.'

'I don't. Well, not in the way you mean it, although I do think that everyone has a duty to contribute in whatever way they can.' She looked him squarely in the eyes. 'Obviously you disagree with that, don't you, Stephen?'

'Because I have chosen to go into private practice rather than work for the NHS?' He gave a short laugh, not sure that he appreciated her making assumptions like that.

'Yes. Oh, I'm not decrying the fact that people should have a choice when it comes to their health care and that those who are able and willing to pay should be allowed to do so. However, the idea that there should be two levels of care is abhorrent to me. Everyone should have equal access to the best treatment available, no matter what their financial circumstances are!'

'And you think that I don't agree with those sentiments?' Stephen asked flatly, incredibly hurt that she should hold such a poor opinion of him. He turned to look towards the river, afraid that she would see how he felt.

'No! I think that deep down you feel the same as I do, Stephen!' Her impassioned voice captured his attention and he turned to look at her again. She gave him a tentative smile.

'I just think that you've allowed the past to influence you,' she said softly. She gave a rueful laugh. 'Before you arrived I had you summed up, you see. I'd met doctors like you before, ones who'd opted for a comfortable life in private practice and everything that went with it—money and prestige to name just two of the benefits.'

'And do I fit this image you had of me?' He gave a deep laugh, determined not to let her see how much her answer mattered to him. 'Don't be shy, Alex. This is tell-the-truth time!'

'No. You aren't what I expected at all, Stephen.' She avoided looking at him so that it was impossible to tell if it had been meant as a compliment or what. 'However, I'm very much afraid that you'll allow the past to influence any decisions you make. I know how hard it must have been when you were growing up, but don't let it rule your life, Stephen.'

'The past influences all of us, Alex, even you. Isn't your decision to work in a practice like Graham's a reaction against your privileged upbringing?' His tone was harsher than it should have been because it stung to realise that he cared so much what she thought of him.

'Oh, you might believe this is what you want to do with your life now, but who's to say things won't change? How long will it be before the novelty wears off and you begin to hanker after the luxuries you're used to?'

He gave her a thin smile although the thought made him flinch inwardly even though he felt compelled to mention it. 'How long will it be before you want to be with people of your own kind, like Simon Ross, for instance? Maybe it's already begun because you two spend a lot of time together.'

'My friendship with Simon isn't the issue here!' she shot back. Stephen struggled to hide his delight as he realised what she had said. So she and Ross were just friends, were they? It answered one question which had been niggling away at him. However, he had no time to dwell on it as she continued.

'But you're wrong if you think that I'll grow tired of this job. I had plenty of other offers but working in the inner city was what I've always wanted to do because I felt that I could make a real contribution to people's lives here.

'It isn't just a whim. If there's one thing my *upbringing* taught me it was how to make up my mind. I learned very early on to stand on my own two feet and not rely on other people. I had to. My parents were hardly ever around and staff changed so often it was hard to remember their names. I know that I won't ever regret the decision I made to work here!'

The angry note in her voice was unmistakable and Stephen bit back a sigh. He certainly hadn't intended to upset her when they were supposed to be having a pleasant day out.

'Then let's just hope that things work out the way we both want them to,' he suggested to smooth things over.

'Meaning that you still intend going back to your own practice? So, what about Graham? Doesn't it worry you how disappointed he's going to be?' she shot back.

He smiled thinly, wishing she'd let the matter drop. He felt a small stab of pain as he recalled what she'd said about having to stand on her own two feet. What a lonely childhood it must have been with only hired help to care for her. No wonder she was so wary about letting down her defences. She'd never had the security of knowing that she'd been loved, as he'd had. Suddenly he realised how lucky he had been to have had his mother there in his formative years, offering unconditional love and support.

'I'm sure that Graham doesn't expect me to stay on. He knows I'm only helping out on a temporary basis,' he said quietly, sobered by the realisation.

'Have you asked him?' she demanded.

'No. But I know Graham and he knows me,' he replied shortly, suddenly wondering if that was true. Was he sure that Graham didn't expect him to take on the new post? Was he sure that he didn't want it even? Suddenly nothing seemed cut and dried any more.

The thought troubled him. He turned to check that Danny was all right as he mulled it over. He returned Danny's wave then let his gaze move on to the river as he sought to drive out the uncertainties their conversation had aroused. He frowned as he spotted the rowing boat he'd noticed earlier heading towards the weir. From where he sat, it appeared that it had gone past the sign warning people of the danger.

He got to his feet in concern, aware of Alex's look of surprise.

'What is it?' she demanded, getting up as well, then gasped in dismay as she saw what he was looking at. 'That boat is heading for the weir!'

'Looks like it.' Stephen glanced round as he heard a shout from further along the bank and saw the man in charge of the boats waving frantically to the family. He managed to attract their attention but the boat had already been caught in the current as the water surged towards the weir.

'They're not going to be able to stop,' Alex exclaimed as she watched the boat being drawn ever closer to the danger.

'I doubt it,' Stephen agreed grimly, setting off at a run towards the river. Other people had been attracted by the shouting so that a crowd was gathering fast. The man who had been rowing had managed to catch hold of a low-lying branch and was clinging on grimly, his wife and children calling for help as the current tried to drag them towards the frothing torrent just a few yards further downstream.

Stephen swiftly assessed the situation then turned to the elderly boatman. 'We need a rope long enough to reach them. Have you got one?'

'There should be one in the hut.' The old man turned and puffed his way back to the hut while Stephen turned to the crowd.

'Can you join hands and make a chain, with the strongest at the front?'

They quickly formed themselves into a line, with two of the fittest-looking men taking up position next to him. 'Right, we'll try to get a rope out to them. I'll wade into the water and toss it to them if you two can hang onto me so that I don't get swept away.'

The men nodded as the boatman came back with a rope. Stephen waded into the water, with one of the men hanging onto his belt and the other holding firmly onto the first with one hand and to the next person in the chain with the other.

'I'm going to throw you this rope,' he shouted.

The man in the rowing boat shouted that he understood, delegating his wife to catch the rope while he clung to the branch. The water tugging at Stephen's legs made it difficult to remain upright but he managed it somehow. The first couple of throws missed but the third landed squarely on target, and a cheer went up from the crowd as the woman managed to fasten it to a ring in the stern.

'Right, haul it in…slowly!' Stephen instructed the crowd,

hardly daring to watch as the boat began to move slowly towards the bank. It was almost within reach when it seemed to snag on something at the bottom of the river, rocking wildly from side to side as the family screamed in terror.

Stephen wasn't sure what happened then because all he saw was one of the children, a little girl, being flung into the water. He acted instinctively as he dived in after her, breaking the surface several yards downstream. He could see the child's head bobbing up and down a few yards ahead and struck out towards her, but there wasn't time to get to her before they were at the weir.

He sucked in a huge breath then tried to relax as the water swept him over the edge. His lungs were burning when he came to the surface again but he didn't have time to worry about how he felt. He could see the little girl floating face down a few yards away and struck out towards her. He was exhausted when he reached the riverbank at last and was glad of the helping hands that dragged him out of the water.

'Are you all right?'

Suddenly Alex was there, the fear he could see in her eyes as she knelt beside him instantly warming him. He touched her cheek in the lightest of caresses yet one which sent a surge of awareness rushing through his body. 'I'm fine,' he said huskily. 'The child…?'

Her voice was almost as husky as his had been. 'Leave her to me, Stephen. You've done your bit.'

Stephen closed his eyes as he took a huge breath. He needed it badly and not just because of the ducking he'd had. There had been something in Alex's eyes when she'd looked at him which made his heart hammer as he recalled it.

She would have been as concerned for anyone in similar circumstances, he told himself, but it didn't work. Alex had been concerned for him, Stephen Spencer, and it felt good to know that…it felt very good indeed!

CHAPTER TEN

'ANYTHING yet?' Stephen shook the perspiration out of his eyes as he glanced up.

'Nothing,' Alex affirmed quietly.

'Then we carry on.' He settled back to the task of resuscitating the little girl, closing his mind to the exhaustion he felt in every battered and bruised inch of his body. How long had they been doing this? he wondered as Alex breathed into the child's mouth again. It had to be a good fifteen minutes at least and they'd carry on for another fifteen or even thirty if that was what it took!

He continued the rhythm—five chest compressions then one breath, another five and another breath, another check to see if there was a pulse. The crowd had fallen silent as they watched, the only sound that of the quiet weeping of the little girl's mother and brother. The father was too shocked to cry, sitting pale and shaking a short distance from the group.

'Wait!' The urgency in Alex's voice broke his concentration and he paused. Sweat was running between his shoulder blades and his ribs were aching, as though someone had played football with them. He rested his hands on his thighs, almost too exhausted to feel anything as she gave a cry of delight.

'We've got a pulse!' She'd barely got the words out before the little girl coughed and brought up a mouthful of water. Deftly rolling the child onto her side, Alex knelt beside her, speaking soothingly as she began to cry.

'It's all right, poppet. You're going to be fine now... That's it. You get rid of all that nasty water.'

'Amy! Oh, Amy...thank God!' The child's mother was sobbing as she knelt down beside her. Alex moved aside to give

them room. She glanced at Stephen and her eyes were dark
with concern.

'Are you OK?'

'Ask me that in half an hour's time.' He managed to smile
but he guessed it didn't fool her. Every bone in his body hurt
from where he'd been bashed against the concrete steps of the
weir and it was a miracle that nothing had been broken. It was
a relief when they heard an ambulance siren and he realised
that his part would be over soon.

Little Amy was fully conscious by the time the paramedics
loaded her on board. She looked very small and frail, tucked
up on the stretcher with an oxygen mask over her nose and
mouth, but she would certainly recover. Stephen shook his head
as her parents struggled to express their gratitude.

'I'm only glad that you were all right at the end of the day,'
he assured them, shaking the father's hand and accepting the
kiss the mother gave him. He sighed as he watched the ambulance driving off. 'For a time back there I didn't think we
were going to save her.'

'Neither did I,' Alex said quietly beside him.

He felt the shudder which ran through her and it seemed the
most natural thing in the world to put his arms around her. He
drew her close, his chin resting on the top of her head as he
took a deep breath. It felt so good, just holding her this way,
as though he had come home after a long and tiring journey.
The thought shook him so that his voice wasn't quite steady
when he spoke.

'Are you all right?'

'I think so.' She let him hold her for a moment longer then
stepped out of his arms as Danny came hurrying over to them.
The little boy could hardly contain his excitement as he skipped
along beside them as they went to the car. He seemed blissfully
unaware of the tragedy which had nearly occurred and for that
Stephen was grateful. He didn't want Danny having nightmares
about it.

They dropped Danny off at Dorothy's and Rita's flat, leaving him to tell the women what had gone on that afternoon. Stephen was starting to feel decidedly uncomfortable now that the bruising was setting in. It was a relief when they got back to the house and he was able to unclip the seat belt which had been pressing against his sore ribs.

He eased himself out of the seat, trying to stifle a groan as every battered inch protested. Alex frowned as she saw his expression. 'Are you OK?'

'Just a bit stiff,' he assured her with massive understatement. However, once inside the house he realised that it would be foolish to ignore what his body was trying to tell him.

'I think I'll have a bath, if you don't mind. I'm feeling a bit stiff and a hot soak should help.'

'Of course I don't mind!' she shot back, glaring at him. 'There's no need to try acting the macho hero with me, Stephen!'

'I wasn't aware that was what I was doing,' he replied coldly, irritated by her attitude because he didn't understand it. He went straight upstairs, wondering what had got into her. She'd sounded really annoyed but he had no idea what was wrong.

He sighed as he turned on the taps. So what was new? Working out what Alex was thinking, it wasn't something he was particularly good at, it seemed!

A long, hot soak did the trick, easing a lot of the stiffness from his aching muscles as well as relaxing his mind. He dried himself off then wrapped a towel around his waist for the short walk to his bedroom, only to come to an abrupt halt in the doorway as he discovered Alex in the room.

She looked round, colour flooding her face as she saw him. 'I…I heard the bath emptying so I brought you this,' she explained in a husky little voice which made every hair on his body stand to attention.

She pointed to the cup and saucer on the bedside table, her

eyes skittering over him before moving quickly away so that Stephen was instantly conscious of the fact that he was standing there wearing nothing more than a scrap of towelling around his hips.

'Thank you.' His voice grated simply because the effort of trying to control his feelings was proving too great. It wasn't the first time he'd been nearly naked in the presence of a woman but it was the first time he'd been around Alex in this state!

He shifted uncomfortably as his body made its own pro-nouncement on that idea and rushed into speech to distract her in case there were any visible signs. 'It was good of you to go to so much trouble,' he said, going over to the chest of drawers and thankfully turning his back on her as he picked up a comb and ran it through his wet hair.

'It's only a cup of coffee, for heaven's sake!'

He looked round as he heard the explosive note in her voice. 'Is there something wrong?' he asked, then could have bitten his tongue as a possible answer surfaced. Had she realised the effect she was having on him? Heaven forbid!

'Yes...no... Damn you, Stephen Spencer, don't you know that you could have been killed today?' She glared at him. 'Yet you stand there, *thanking* me for a cup of coffee!'

'But I wasn't killed.' He tossed the comb onto the chest, barely able to conceal his relief that he'd been wrong. 'I'm fine, Alex, honestly. A bit bruised and battered but otherwise perfectly all right.'

'I... You...' She pressed a hand to her mouth to stifle a sob, which stunned him when he heard it. Swinging round, she rushed towards the door, but somehow he managed to get there ahead of her. He wasn't sure what was happening and didn't waste time working it out as he caught her in his arms and turned her round, ignoring her attempts to break free.

'Let me go! Damn you, Stephen, don't you hear what I say?' she demanded, glaring up at him with swimming eyes.

'Yes, I hear you, Alex.' He took a deep breath as his heart swelled with sudden excitement. Maybe he was misreading the situation once again but suddenly he knew that was a chance he had to take. 'I hear the words but do you mean them?'

His voice was slow and deliberate so there could be no mistaking what he was saying. 'Do you really want me to let you go?'

'I... No!' He wasn't sure which of them moved first. Maybe he bent towards her or perhaps she came up to meet him, but suddenly their mouths met in a kiss which was as clumsy as it was earth-shattering. Their need was simply too great to waste time worrying about technique. There was just the hot, wild pressure of Alex's lips beneath his, the hunger which ran so rawly through his veins, and he suddenly made sense of everything that had been a mystery before. He loved her. It was as simple as that.

He made a rough sound deep in his throat as his arms tightened so she was locked against him from breast to thigh. The damp folds of towelling were no barrier and he knew that she could feel the betraying pressure of his body against the softness of hers by the way she tensed...

She relaxed against him, letting him draw her closer until they were as close as two people could be without the ultimate act of togetherness.

Stephen was overwhelmed by the force of his feelings. It wasn't just this hunger he felt to make love to Alex but a deep tenderness as well. He wanted to love her and cherish her, set her body on fire and yet soothe her when she needed soothing. He'd never realised that loving someone involved so many complex emotions. It was going to be a new and wonderful experience, learning them all.

His mouth gentled at the thought, shifting until it found a new, enticing way to mate with hers. This kiss was far less forceful but none the less potent because of that. He felt the shudder that ran through her body and into his, and smiled against her mouth in pleasure. Did loving entail sharing even the smallest things, like a shiver? He had no experience to draw on but he was looking forward to finding out.

'What are you smiling about?' She drew back, a frown puckering her brow as she looked into his face. Stephen smoothed away the tiny lines with his lips then let them drift back to the enticing curve of hers.

'Nothing…everything,' he murmured as his mouth settled over hers once more, and he felt *her* smile at that. It was a crazy answer but, then, he felt crazy, crazy and wonderfully alive, full of his newly discovered love for her.

Her soft gasp of delight as his lips opened hers so that his tongue could slide between them was another joy to be savoured, as was the taste of her. Stephen groaned as he held her closer, his hand moving upwards to cup her breast, his pulse leaping as he felt her nipple peaking through the thickness of her sweater. When he felt her hands slide around his waist to caress the strong lines of his back, he shuddered. Suddenly he couldn't stand it any longer and knew that he had to touch her without the barrier of clothing before he went crazy!

He slid his hands beneath her sweater then stilled as he felt her stiffen. His eyes flew to her face and he felt his heart plummet as he saw the uncertainty there. Surely Alex didn't think this was wrong? It seemed inconceivable to him after the rawness of those kisses they'd just shared.

'Alex?' His voice was gentle despite the fear he felt.

'There…there's something I should tell you, Stephen.' Her voice was so low that he had to strain to hear it, even though there wasn't another sound in the room. He felt her take a quick breath and struggled to contain a rush of desire as her breasts brushed his bare chest. It made his head spin so that he had difficulty following what she was saying.

'What was that?' he murmured, sure that he couldn't have heard her correctly.

'I said that I have never slept with anyone before.' She gave a sharp little laugh, a mixture of embarrassment and defiance as she felt him stiffen. 'I know it seems unbelievable that a woman of my age is…is still a virgin, but it's true.'

Well, she certainly knew how to disconcert him! Stephen's reeling mind reeled a bit more as he absorbed what she was telling him. On the one hand he was filled with elation at the thought that no other man had made love to her, while on the other he wondered about the reason for it. He knew that he had to find out before things went any further.

He set her gently away from him, not sure he'd have the strength to hold out much longer if he didn't remove temptation from his reach.

'There must have been a reason for that, Alex?'

'There was.' She looked him straight in the eye. 'My parents made no secret of the fact that they were both having affairs. I don't suppose they realised that I knew what was going on but I couldn't help but be aware of it. I also knew how unhappy my mother was.

'Oh, she kept up a front but deep down I knew she was only trying to pay my father back because she was so hurt by the way he treated her. I don't think he ever really loved her, you see. My mother is a beautiful and talented woman, she fitted the bill as the perfect wife for a man of his standing, which is why, I suspect, he married her. Maybe it seems idealistic but I made myself promise that I would never make the same mistake. I wouldn't sleep with a man until I was certain that I was in love with him and that he was in love with me.'

And she wasn't in love with him, Stephen thought sickly. That was what she was telling him. Oh, she might have enjoyed kissing him, might even have been tempted to take things further, but she wasn't in love with him and there was no way that she would compromise her principles.

'I see. And I understand.' He moved away so that she couldn't see the devastation he felt. He loved her! But what was the point of telling her that when she didn't feel the same way about him? It would only embarrass them both. It would be far better if he glossed over what had happened, by treating it as nothing more than an understandable lapse.

'Not to worry.' Somehow he managed to smile even though it felt as though his heart were breaking into hundreds of tiny sharp splinters. 'I think you're right to know what you want, Alex, and to stick to it. Far too many people jump into bed for the wrong reasons and then regret it later.'

'As we would have done?' she queried a shade bitterly. Stephen frowned, wondering what had caused that note in her voice, but it was impossible to tell and pointless to ask. She had made it perfectly clear how she felt. Surely he didn't need to know anything else?

She gave him a cool smile as she went to the door. 'Let's just put what happened down to the drama of the day, shall we? I imagine that's the real explanation for it.'

Stephen sank down on the bed after she'd left and put his head in his hands. If only that were the explanation! But that Alex could dismiss it as such made him grateful that he hadn't made a complete fool of himself. He could just imagine her reaction if he'd blurted out that he was in love with her!

He got slowly to his feet and started to dress. The sooner he could get away from this situation the better. It had been a mistake, coming back here…a very big mistake indeed!

'I don't know how I can thank you for all you've done…' Debbie Francis's voice broke and Stephen patted her hand. It was almost two weeks since he'd taken Danny to the river, two of the longest weeks of his life. The only way he'd got through them was by filling every waking hour with work.

From writing to the area health authority about the Factor VIII problem to agreeing to help set up the new residents' committee, Stephen had thrown himself into every project which had come up. It had filled his waking hours but the nights had been more difficult to get through…

'It's good to see you making such an excellent recovery,' he said quickly to cover the all too familiar pain. 'It must feel great, being back home at last.'

'Oh, it is!' Debbie assured him. 'I missed Danny so much, although he doesn't appear to have missed me half as much! Rita was marvellous, the way she looked after him like that, and you and Dr Campbell, of course. He told me that you'd taken him to your flat and everything.'

'It was nothing.' Stephen stood up, not wanting to be reminded of that day. Time and again he'd gone over what had happened that evening in his room, although he knew that it was pointless. Alex had made it clear how she felt. She didn't love him. It was as simple, and as painful, as that.

'Well, I'd better get on,' he said briskly, closing his mind to the stabbing pain he was having to learn to live with. 'I've a list of people to see this afternoon and then I promised to drop in to see Dr Barker. He's out of hospital, did you know?'

'Yes, Rita told me.' Debbie smiled as she got carefully up from the chair. The operation to relieve the pressure on her brain caused by a blood clot had been one hundred per cent successful, but she was going to need time to recover her strength. 'She also told me that Dr Barker is staying with Meg while he recuperates. Do I detect a hint of romance in the air?'

Stephen laughed. 'Let's hope so! They're both such nice people that they seem made for one another, don't they?'

'They do. It would be nice to know that Dr Barker has something to look forward to when he retires. I saw the item in the paper about the new health centre,' she explained. 'It sounds marvellous but I can't imagine that Dr Barker will be fit enough to take on such a huge undertaking at his age. Still, he's got the perfect replacement, hasn't he?'

Stephen merely smiled because there was little he could say other than to state that he wouldn't be going after the post. That would only lead to questions and he certainly didn't want to go into his reasons for not wanting it.

He bade Debbie goodbye then went down in the lift, thinking how his objections had changed in the past four weeks. Now he didn't want the job because working with Alex for any prolonged period would have been too painful. It had little to do with his earlier views about not wanting to work in the area or give up his own practice. Frankly, he couldn't see himself going back there.

The realisation shocked him so that he didn't notice the lift had stopped. He didn't want to go back to his former life. It was as simple as that. Working here, he had found the things which had been missing before—a sense of purpose and the satisfaction of knowing that he was making a difference. Status and money were no longer important to him. He didn't need them any more because he had exorcised his ghosts and found his place, and that place was here.

Or somewhere very like it, he amended quickly. Staying in this area, that was out of the question in the circumstances. Coming into daily contact with Alex would be too painful now, but if things had been different...

He sighed as he stepped out of the lift. There was no point in wishing for something he couldn't have!

Stephen finished his calls then dropped in to see Graham on his way home, delighted by how well his old friend was looking. Whether it was the result of the operation or Meg's attentive care, it was certainly paying off. Graham seemed to have shed a good ten years in the few weeks since he'd visited Stephen at his surgery that day.

'Come on in. Tea?' Graham offered, leading the way into the cosy living-room of the small flat above the nursing home.

'Thanks. I'd love some.' Stephen sat down as Graham bustled into the kitchen. 'No need to ask how you are, I see.'

Graham poked his head round the door and smiled. 'I feel great. Meg and I are thinking of going on holiday once I get the all-clear—just a few days in the Lakes to do a spot of walking. It's been ages since I felt up to it.'

'Sounds a great idea,' Stephen endorsed. He scooped a pile of newspapers off the coffee-table as Graham brought the cups back. 'Thanks.'

'Meg suggested it.' Graham smiled reflectively. 'She's a wonderful person, so warm and caring.'

'I got the impression she feels much the same way about you.' Stephen looked pointedly at the older man and heard him laugh self-consciously.

'Is it *that* obvious how I feel about her? I never thought I'd ever feel like this again, to tell the truth. There's been my work, you see, and that was more than enough for me.'

'But things have changed?' Stephen grinned. 'And why shouldn't they? Come on, Graham, it's time you started thinking about yourself for once! Don't you dare feel guilty.'

'I don't! It sounds crazy to say it but it's true. If I could just be certain that I had the right person to take over from me…' He put his cup down abruptly. 'There's no point beating about the bush any longer, Stephen. You know what I'm trying to say, don't you?'

'Yes.' Stephen stood up, unable to remain seated any longer. 'You want me to apply for the post as director of the new health centre.' He shook his head. 'It's out of the question, Graham. I'm sorry.'

'Why?' Graham held up his hand when Stephen went to muster the old arguments. 'I know what you're going to say. You have your own practice and you wanted to escape from here. Do you think I don't understand how you felt, Stephen? But things have changed, haven't they? *You've* changed.'

'I don't know what you mean,' Stephen denied shortly, walking to the window to stare along the road.

'Don't you? There was no need for you to get involved with the health authority over Danny, neither did you have to help set up the residents' committee.' He saw the start Stephen gave and laughed ruefully. 'Alex has told me all about it.'

'Has she?' He saw Graham frown at the bite in his voice and turned away again. 'Perhaps, but she got it out of context. I couldn't sit around, doing nothing. It filled in a few hours, getting involved with those things, that's all.'

'Is it?' Graham picked up his cup again. 'It seems I was wrong, then, doesn't it? So, when are you going back to your own place? Meg and I were hoping to get away this weekend, but if you're eager to leave we can easily change our plans.'

'There's no need,' Stephen said quickly, hating himself for the way his heart plummeted at the idea of leaving so soon. What did he hope to achieve by staying? a small voice taunted. Alex wasn't interested in him; she most certainly wasn't in love with him!

It took him all his time to keep the pain out of his voice. 'I promised you that I'd stay for six weeks and that's what I'll do.'

'Fine.' Graham's smile was faintly smug. 'Another couple of weeks should sort things out nicely.'

He was referring to his coming holiday and his romance with Meg, Stephen told himself. But when he left the nursing home he still wasn't convinced. He sighed as he got into his car. Did Graham honestly think that two weeks would make a difference to his decision?

Why not? that voice piped up again. Look how four weeks has changed your whole outlook.

'Oh, shut up!' Stephen ordered aloud, starting the car with a roar which at another time would have made him wince. That day it didn't seem to matter. In fourteen days he would be leaving. That he would probably never see Alex again after that was a thought destined to give him more sleepless nights!

CHAPTER ELEVEN

'I APPRECIATE you dropping in to see me, Mrs Bashir. And I'm delighted that you're feeling so much better than the last time we met.'

Stephen smiled as Darla quickly translated what he'd said for her mother's benefit. Morning surgery had just finished when the two women had arrived to see him. Stephen wasn't sure why they had come, but he suspected that there was another reason behind the visit apart from a desire on Mrs Bashir's part to thank him. He waited patiently as she said something to her daughter, frowning when Darla shook her head vehemently.

'Is there something wrong, Darla?' he asked, and saw the nervous look the teenager shot him.

'Of course not—' she began, but her mother interrupted in halting English.

'My child does not want me to speak to you,' Mrs Bashir said painstakingly. 'She believes it will make...' She stopped, turning to her daughter for the word she needed.

'Trouble,' Darla supplied unhappily, and Mrs Bashir nodded.

'Yes...trouble.' She broke off again, turning beseechingly to the teenager once more. Stephen realised how difficult it must be for her and waited patiently, although he couldn't help wondering what was going on.

He didn't have long to wait, however, because all of a sudden Darla seemed to make up her mind. 'My mother wanted to come here to see if you can do anything to help my sister. She is living with us at the moment, with her husband and son, because she is too scared to go back to her own flat.'

Darla's dark eyes were full of fear. 'That Richardson boy

159

has threatened to hurt her baby if she and Ranji go home, and this is why she is so frightened, you see.'

'You mean Darren Richardson?' Stephen sighed when the girl nodded. 'Has your sister been to the police?'

'Not recently. She is afraid to do that. The police try but each time that Darren Richardson has an alibi.' Darla shrugged unhappily. 'I told my mother that you wouldn't be able to do anything but she insisted on coming.'

'I certainly can't promise anything. However, I shall have a word with the police and make sure they are aware of the situation. I'll also contact the local housing department—threatening other tenants is something they take a very strong view about.'

'But that will only make things worse!' Darla cried, sounding really scared. 'If Darren finds out that we have reported him there is no knowing what he could do!'

'Surely the alternative—sitting back and letting him get away with it—is worse?' Stephen said quickly, but it was obvious that she wasn't convinced. She rapidly translated what he'd said for her mother's benefit then they both got up to leave.

He saw them out, sighing as he watched them walking down the drive. Something had to be done about this situation. It went totally against the grain to allow people's lives to be ruined because of such bullying tactics!

'Stephen?'

He felt a shiver ripple down his spine as he heard Alex's voice. He was glad he had his back to her because it gave him time to pull himself together before he turned. She was standing in the office doorway, holding a letter in her hand. The glow from the electric light overhead set fire to her red hair, creating a blazing numbus of colour around it.

Stephen felt the full force of his feelings hit him almost like a physical blow. He loved her so much it seemed inconceivable that she didn't love him in return. Yet he had only to look at the cool expression on her face to know that his feelings most certainly weren't reciprocated.

'Yes? Do you want me?' he asked in a voice that was mercifully devoid of feeling.

'If you could spare a moment I'd be grateful,' she replied just as blandly.

He went back along the corridor, glancing into the waiting-room as he passed the door. There were no more patients, waiting to be seen, and Dorothy was clearing up the toys and magazines so that the place would be tidy for the evening.

She smiled as she spotted him. 'You've not forgotten about this afternoon, I hope?'

'Sorry?' Stephen frowned uncomprehendingly.

'Elsie Jones's birthday party.' Dorothy sighed. 'Really, Stephen, you should have remembered that, you being guest of honour!'

He managed not to groan. The last thing he felt like at the moment was partying! 'What time are we expected?'

'Three o'clock. Alex is going to cover this afternoon's calls, aren't you, love?'

'Yes. It's no problem,' she assured him when he glanced at her for confirmation. 'There are only a few for once so I might even get a chance to come on to the party after I finish.'

'Fine. Thanks.' Stephen frowned. 'Is that what you wanted to speak to me about?'

'No. I had this back from the hospital today. It's the result of Letitia Churchill's jejunal biopsy. It is tropical sprue, as you suspected.'

She handed him the note. Stephen read it through, before passing it back to her. 'I'm glad we were on the right track.'

'Less of "we" and more of "you",' Alex stated emphatically. She glanced at Dorothy, before turning to him again, and there was a sudden seriousness about her expression which made his heart leap painfully. 'Do you think we could have a word...in private?'

'Of course.' He followed her to her room, waiting while she closed the door. His heart was hammering so fast that it felt as though it were going to burst right out of his chest as he wondered what she needed to talk to him about…

He clamped down on the thought that sprang to mind. Alex wasn't about to declare that she was madly, passionately in love with him! He could get that idea right out of his head.

'Look, Stephen, there isn't an easy way to say this so I may as well get straight to the point. I've decided to hand in my notice.'

Well, she'd certainly got his attention! Stephen stared at her, making no attempt to hide his surprise. 'Why?'

'Because it would be the best thing for everyone.' She went over to the window and stood with her back towards him, but he could tell by the ramrod stiffness of her spine that she was finding this difficult. His stomach churned as though he'd stepped into a lift and dropped ten floors, but he couldn't leave it at that—he had to find out why she'd made such a decision.

'Best for whom?' he asked shortly. 'You, me, Graham, the patients? Can you be a bit more specific here, Alex?'

His tone was patronising and he could tell by the angry look she shot him that she didn't take kindly to it. 'For everyone. You, me, Graham *and* the patients.'

'I find that hard to believe!' His tone was acerbic. 'How can you leaving improve things when you know this practice is stretched beyond any sensible limits as it is?'

'Because if I leave you might decide to stay!' she snapped back, taking the wind right out of his sails again. 'Look, Stephen, I'm not blind. I've seen how much you've changed since coming here. When Graham first hinted that he wanted you to take over the new health centre I thought he was mad.'

'Thank you,' he said sardonically. 'Not that it comes as a surprise. You made your feelings plain from the moment I arrived!'

She flushed at that. 'I know I did. And I apologise for it. I think I explained to you that I had a preconceived idea of what you would be like, and that I quickly realised I'd been wrong. I now believe that you are the best person for the job and that Graham was right all along.'

'There's just one small flaw in all this,' he said, struggling not to let her see how that had affected him. He had wanted so much for her opinion of him to improve that it was like being handed a gift to hear her admitting it. However, he couldn't afford to become too euphoric until he knew all the facts. 'I'm not sure that I want the post.'

'Oh, come on, Stephen! Why cut off your nose to spite your face?' A smile suddenly softened her mouth. 'You know very well that you love working here. You wouldn't be putting so much into the job if you didn't!'

He shifted uncomfortably. 'I pride myself on doing a good job.'

'But this is more than just a *job*, isn't it?' Her tone became gentle, making his nerves tauten in immediate response, yet she seemed mercifully unaware of the effect she was having. 'You really care about the people around here. You wouldn't have taken on the area health authority over Danny's treatment or set up the residents' committee if you didn't, so don't try to deny it. Nor would people like Neelam Bashir be coming to you for help if she didn't know how you felt.'

He shrugged, still not wanting to admit that she might be right. 'It isn't in my nature to sit back and do nothing.'

'Maybe not. But I've watched you, Stephen, seen how day by day you've been drawn into their lives. I know, even if you won't admit it, that you care. And that's why I'm going to tell Graham that I'm leaving.'

'But why? I don't understand—' he began, but she interrupted him.

'Because of what happened between us. Do you think I haven't realised what a...a strain it's put on our working relationship?'

His heart turned over. What did she mean? Had Alex realised that he was in love with her, was that what she was telling him—that she couldn't work with him if he did decide to apply for the post because she would find the situation intolerable?

He was sure that was the explanation and he didn't know what to say, but she saved him from having to think of anything by giving a small, knowing laugh which only managed to make him feel even worse.

'So I was right. In which case, the only option open to me is to hand in my notice. I couldn't live with myself if I deprived the people in this area of a wonderful doctor by my own selfishness!'

She quickly left the room, but for a long time after she'd gone Stephen remained where he was. He'd known all along that Alex didn't love him but at the back of his mind there had been a glimmer of hope that he might be able to make her fall in love with him. Now that hope had been snuffed out and it felt as though he had been dropped into a huge black pit where no light or warmth could ever reach him. Alex didn't love him and never would. How could he bear to carry on, knowing that?

'Come in, Stephen. Your date is awaiting you!'

Meg Parker opened the door to his knock, smiling as she looked him up and down. 'Mmm, I hope we've got enough smelling salts on hand. There are going to be quite a few of our ladies having the vapours when they get a look at you. You've really done Elsie proud!'

Stephen smiled, as was expected of him, struggling to hide the heavy weight which seemed to have lodged in his chest since the conversation with Alex that lunchtime. Given the choice, he wouldn't have come, but he knew how disappointed Elsie would have been if he hadn't turned up. Now he glanced ruefully down at the dinner suit he was wearing, complete with starched white shirt and bow-tie.

'Not too over the top, I hope? Dorothy warned me that I had to dress the part.'

'You look perfect! Wait until you see Elsie and you'll see what I mean.'

Meg led the way to the communal lounge and opened the door with a flourish. Stephen paused to take in the scene that greeted him. The room had been decorated with brightly coloured balloons and streamers, the chairs pushed back against the walls to leave the central area for dancing. There was quite a crowd there, guests as well as residents, and all were dressed in their finery, he was pleased to see. At least he wasn't the odd man out!

''Ere 'e is. Ooh, ain't he gorgeous?' Elsie came hobbling towards him, smiling her toothy smile as Stephen offered her the corsage of gardenias he'd brought for her. 'For me, Dr Spencer?' she asked with a catch in her voice.

'Of course. Although it's a bit like gilding the lily. You look quite beautiful enough in that dress, Mrs Jones,' he assured her, taking an admiring look at the long emerald green dress— heavily adorned with sequins—she was wearing while he pushed aside the memory of when that comparison had last sprung to mind, the first time he'd seen Alex.

He wasn't going to think about Alex for the next hour, he told himself. He would keep her right out of his mind, but he knew that it was going to be a herculean task.

'Green was my Sidney's favourite colour,' the old lady told him, preening. 'Always said as it suited me a treat, 'e did.'

'He was right, too,' Stephen assured her. He glanced round as Meg offered him a cup of fruit punch. 'Thanks.'

'Non-alcoholic,' she informed him *sotto voce*. 'Not a good idea to mix alcohol with the medication most of our residents are on…not that they know that. They think it's spiked with all sorts of naughty things!'

Stephen laughed as he took a sip. 'Should be a lively do, then!' He let Elsie lead him over to her friends and family, replying pleasantly to the introductions. Grandson Barry was there and he gave Stephen a broad wink.

'Gran's been beside herself, waiting for you to arrive, Doc,' he informed him. He grinned as someone put on some music. 'There'll be no stopping her now!'

Stephen laughed as he handed Barry his fruit punch as the old lady claimed him to dance with her. 'I just hope I can remember how to do this! It's been years since I waltzed…!'

By the time Meg and some of the other staff brought in the teatrays Stephen was ready for a breather. Not to be outdone, several of the other residents had claimed him to partner them, and the effort of steering stiff, elderly bodies around the dance floor had been tiring, to say the least. Still, it had helped take his mind off other things, or it had until Graham drew him aside.

'Alex has just told me that she's handing in her notice,' Graham informed him without any preamble. 'She said that you already knew about it. What's going on, Stephen? It's the last thing I expected!'

'It's her decision.' He shrugged, feeling a wave of heat rush through his veins as the door opened and Alex came in. She had changed in honour of the occasion and looked so lovely in a sleeveless mint green dress, worn with high-heeled sandals, that Stephen forgot what he'd been going to say. It was only as he realised that Graham was watching him that he struggled on.

'I'm sure she explained her reasons for wanting to leave,' he said flatly, turning away so that he wouldn't have to watch her crossing the room to give Elsie her present.

'Oh, she gave me a reason, something about wanting to broaden her horizons and that she was thinking of going overseas to work. Evidently, Simon Ross is going out to Africa to work for the WHO and Alex is thinking of going along as well. Did you know?'

'No. I had no idea,' Stephen replied, striving to control the pain he felt. Alex had made no mention of that when they'd spoken that morning. Why not?

His heart sank as the explanation came to him in a flash. She hadn't told him her plans because she'd realised how hurt he'd be to learn that they involved another man. She must be aware that Stephen was in love with her—she had to be when that was the reason she was leaving! But she'd tried to spare his feelings. It made him feel even more wretched because he felt so humiliated.

'Well, I think she's making a mistake!' Graham sounded unaccustomedly angry and Stephen glanced at him in concern. Although Graham had made an excellent recovery, Stephen didn't want the older man getting upset about this.

'Maybe you can change her mind,' he suggested quietly, his mind racing. If he made it clear to Alex that he had no intention of going after the post at the new health centre, there would be no reason for her to leave.

'I already tried that.' Graham sighed ruefully. 'It's pure selfishness, I expect, wanting her to stay here. All along I had it in mind what a good team you two would make. I just never took into account that Alex might have other plans for the future.' He shrugged, mercifully not looking at Stephen as he added, 'I certainly didn't suspect there was anything between her and Simon Ross but, then, I'd be the first to admit I'm no expert in these matters!'

Stephen didn't say anything because he couldn't trust himself. However, it made him see how pointless it would be, telling Alex he wasn't applying for the new job. Her decision to leave was based on a desire to be with Simon Ross and had nothing to do with him. So much for her assurances that she and Ross were just friends! He should have realised there had been more to it than that.

It was a relief when Meg came over just then and laughingly demanded that Graham dance with her. Most people were having a final turn on the floor now that tea was over. Stephen saw Elsie being led round by Barry, then spotted Dorothy dancing with one of the few gentlemen residents of the nursing home, who had been much in demand that afternoon as a partner. Everyone seemed to be having fun…except him.

His gaze moved on and came to rest on Alex. She was standing by the window and there was a look of such sadness on her face that he couldn't help himself. Of their own volition his feet began moving, yet when he reached her he wasn't sure what to say. How could he ask her what was wrong when she'd made it plain that her feelings weren't any of his business?

He took a deep breath to mask the agony he felt. 'It seems we're both wallflowers so would you like to dance?'

He half expected her to refuse so was surprised when she immediately accepted. 'I'd like that, Stephen. Thank you.'

Her voice was very low so he wondered if that was why he thought he'd heard a break in it. He cast her a quick glance as they moved onto the floor but there was no sign of anything on her face. He bit back a sigh as he took her into his arms. He was attributing his own feelings to her and he would have to stop because it just made things worse.

The music came to an end almost as soon as they started dancing, but someone put the record back on and everyone set off around the floor again with varying degrees of expertise. Stephen held Alex away from him, not trusting himself if he held her too close. It was bad enough to feel the fleeting pressure of her body against his as they made a tight turn to avoid Elsie and Barry.

'Graham just told me about your plans to work overseas,' he said, hurriedly easing her away from him when they had a clear space once more. 'You must be excited about it.'

'Yes. It will be a challenge, won't it?' There wasn't much indication of excitement in her voice, and Stephen frowned.

'What made you decide to take such a step?' he asked.

'I would have thought that was obvious,' she replied with a brittle laugh that grated.

'You mean because Ross is going out there,' he stated bluntly, trying to control the pain that stabbed his heart. He gave a gravelly laugh. 'Funny, but his decision to work for the WHO doesn't gel with the impression I got of him.'

'What do you mean?' Alex frowned as she looked up at him. Stephen felt his heart skip a beat as he stared into her face. She was so beautiful and he loved her so much, yet he was powerless to let her know that, especially now that it was clear another man had laid claim to her heart.

'Only that you told me Ross was noted for his meanness,' he explained flatly, struggling to keep a grip on his emotions. 'Nobody gets rich working for the WHO so it just doesn't seem to fit, that's all.'

She gave a strained laugh. 'It appears that I've been mis-judging Simon. Evidently he's been contributing to the upkeep of a relief centre out in Mozambique and that's why he's been so reluctant to spend any money. Most of what he's earned in the past three years has been ploughed into the project and now he's decided to go over there and put his expertise to good use as well.'

He should have guessed! Not only had Ross captured her heart, he was also on the road to sainthood! Stephen tried to clamp down on the cynical thought but it was useless. It was a relief when the music ended and he could let her go.

'Then I expect he's doubly delighted that you've decided to go over there with him,' he said with a smile that made his face ache from the sheer effort of keeping it in place. 'I'm sure that you and he will make a great team, Alex.'

'I…I'm sure you're right.' There was no mistaking the catch in her voice now, but before Stephen could wonder about it she had moved away. He watched her go over to speak to Elsie, responding with a laugh and shake of her head to something the old lady said…

He didn't wait to see any more. Watching Alex and wishing for the impossible, it was too painful. He went to find Meg and thanked her for the tea, making up some excuse about needing to get back to the surgery to explain why he wasn't able to say his goodbyes to Elsie in person.

Stephen slipped away, unnoticed, to his relief. He hadn't thought he could have felt any worse than he'd felt at lunchtime when Alex had told him of her decision to resign, but he'd been wrong. Knowing that she was planning a future with another man was so painful that he didn't think he'd be able to stand it.

He walked back to the surgery and it felt as though he was walking away from any chance of happiness.

'I wasn't sure what to do! That's why I brought Jodie here. I know surgery has finished, Dr Spencer…'

'It's all right, Donna. Don't worry about that. Come in.' Stephen ushered the teenager along the hall to his consulting room. Evening surgery had ended a good half-hour before. He'd been half-heartedly scouting around the kitchen for something to eat when the bell had rung and he'd found Donna Fielding and her baby on the step. It had been immediately obvious from the girl's face that something was seriously wrong so he didn't waste any time.

'Put Jodie on the couch and tell me what happened,' he instructed. He waited only as long as it took for the teenager to do as he'd said, before starting to examine the baby, and was instantly struck by the way Jodie seemed to have difficulty focusing on him.

Quickly unsnapping the poppers on the baby's pink sleep suit, he examined her tiny body, pausing as he noticed what looked like finger marks forming a band of bruises around her ribcage.

'I don't know what happened!' Donna was almost incoherent with fear. 'I'd been out, you see. I got myself a job down at the transport café—just a couple of hours of a night so I can earn a bit of money to buy things for Jodie. Tracey, who lives in the next flat, usually minds her for me but she was going out tonight so I told Darren he had to do it.'

'I see.' Stephen's tone was grim because he was starting to get an idea what might be wrong with the child. He quickly fetched his torch and checked the baby's eyes, relieved when she responded, albeit sluggishly, to the light. Easing his fingers under her head, he gently checked for any signs of lumps or a depression but couldn't find any. 'So what happened when you got home? Was Jodie like this then?'

'Yes! I went in to see if she was all right, like I always do, and she was just lying in her cot, staring. She…she didn't seem to know I was there, which isn't like her! I asked Darren what had happened but he said she's been asleep the whole time I'd been out, but…but I could tell he was lying!'

A sob shook her. 'He's done something to her, hasn't he, Dr Spencer? Hit her or…or something?'

'It certainly looks as though something has happened to her, Donna,' Stephen agreed softly, feeling anger building inside him. He glanced round as the door suddenly opened and Alex appeared.

'Is everything all right?' she asked, shooting a look at the sobbing Donna and then at the baby on the couch.

'No. Can you phone for an ambulance, please? It looks very much like shaken baby syndrome to me,' he said tersely.

'Right.' She didn't waste time on questions as she put through the call. Her face was very grave as she came to stand by the couch. 'How is she? Does she respond to external stimuli?'

'Yes, thank God!' He couldn't disguise his feelings and he saw her shoot him a quick look before she turned to the sobbing teenager. Donna repeated everything she'd told Stephen, and Alex's expression said it all after the girl had finished her tale.

'I shouldn't have left her with him! It's all my fault…'

Donna was almost beside herself and Alex laid a comforting arm around her shoulders.

'It isn't your fault, Donna. You love Jodie and you look after her really well,' she assured her.

'Then why is she here now? I hate that Darren Richardson! I do! I'll never forgive him if anything happens to Jodie!'

The girl lapsed into a storm of weeping and Stephen was glad when Alex led her away and sat her down at the far side of the room. He didn't want Jodie getting upset by picking up on her mother's distress, although he was glad that the child wasn't so badly injured as to be unaware of what was happening around her.

He looked up as Alex came back, accepting her help as they carefully wrapped the baby in a blanket to maintain her body heat while they waited for the paramedics. 'If I could get my hands on that boy…'

Alex touched his hand. 'I know, Stephen. Somebody will have to put a stop to Darren's antics.'

'And that someone is going to be me!' he said emphatically, moving his hand away because it was too much to bear to have her touch him in view of the circumstances.

He looked round as the doorbell rang, avoiding her eyes in case his face gave him away. 'That will be the ambulance. I'd like to go with Donna, if that's all right with you.'

'Of course. I'm on call tonight anyway, so it makes no difference,' she assured him with an ease that hurt.

Of course it made no difference if he stayed or went, he thought bitterly as he hurried to let the paramedics in. He didn't feature in Alex's life so why should she care one way or the other what he did? And once she'd left the practice, and was heading off to Mozambique with Simon Ross, she wouldn't need to give him another thought. Hell!

CHAPTER TWELVE

IT WAS after midnight by the time Stephen left the hospital, but at least he had the comfort of knowing that Jodie was in safe hands. The consultant who'd been summoned after Stephen had pulled a few strings was an expert in the field of child abuse and had confirmed his initial diagnosis that Jodie had been shaken. A brain scan had shown some minor swelling but everyone was hopeful that it would subside in the next day or so and shouldn't cause any permanent damage.

Stephen had given a statement to the police and had encouraged Donna to tell her side of the story. They were going to follow it up and he only prayed that Darren would get his just desserts. There was simply no excuse for doing that to an innocent child!

He took a taxi home and had it drop him off in the street so as not to disturb Alex if she was asleep. However, she had waited up and came out of the sitting-room to meet him.

'How is she?' she asked, her beautiful face full of concern.

'Stable at present,' he replied flatly, struggling to control the rush of emotions he felt. How was he going to bear knowing that she was on the other side of the world, living with another man? He had no idea, but he was going to have to learn to cope so he might as well make a start right away.

'The consultant is hopeful that no permanent damage has been done, although it's too early to be certain. We'll just have to keep our fingers crossed.' He gave her a brief smile then made his way upstairs before the temptation to linger overruled common sense. It took him only a few minutes to get ready for bed. What Alex was doing he had no idea, and didn't let himself dwell on it. What she did wasn't his concern.

*　　*　　*

'Apparently, the police have had to let him go. He's saying that he didn't hurt the baby and that it's all Donna's fault—'

Dorothy broke off when she saw that Stephen had come into the room. 'I was just telling Alex that it looks as though that Darren Richardson is going to wriggle out of trouble again,' she explained for his benefit.

Stephen frowned. It was three days since baby Jodie had been injured, and although she was making an excellent recovery that didn't mean his anger had lessened in any way. 'Are you sure? It's obvious to anyone that Donna would never hurt that child. What's wrong with the police? Are they blind or something?'

'Their hands are tied, Stephen. Surely you can see that?' Alex shrugged as he shot her an angry look. 'It's Darren's word against Donna's who's to blame.'

'Maybe. But if they took account of all the other evidence they must have on record about that boy, surely their own common sense would show them who the most likely culprit is!' he retorted hotly.

Dorothy quietly excused herself, obviously uncomfortable with the atmosphere in the room. Stephen swung round on his heel, knowing in his heart that he was overreacting. The police would do all they could to get to the bottom of this tragedy but they had guidelines to follow.

He sighed as he went to his room and sat down, even though morning surgery had ended some time before. He needed some time on his own to get to grips with the way he felt. Of course he was angry about what Darren had done to Jodie, but a lot of his anger stemmed from how he felt inside.

It didn't make any difference that he knew it was foolish but he kept trying to think of ways to make Alex stay, and that was what was really upsetting him—the fact that he couldn't think of a single reason to persuade her. She was in love with Simon Ross—what could he come up with to hold sway against that?

By the time Graham phoned an hour later, Stephen had managed to get back on an even keel. It was his free afternoon, although he usually spent it catching up on paperwork. When Graham suggested that he drop by for coffee, he agreed readily enough. He knew what Graham wanted to discuss, of course. Graham wanted to know if he intended applying for the directorship of the new health centre. Maybe it was time he made up his mind.

Graham got straight to the point after coffee had been poured. 'I've been on to the area health authority. They are very interested in you taking on this job, Stephen. Obviously, they have to advertise it, and they are bound to get other people interested. However, they were quite open about the fact that they don't expect to get anyone as highly qualified as you applying for the post. Now all we need to know is whether or not you're interested.'

Stephen took a deep breath. They had reached crunch point! Whatever he decided now would stand because he wouldn't go back on his decision once it had been made. It surprised him just how easy it was in the end.

'Yes, I'm interested in the job. I feel that I could make a go of it, given the chance.'

'That's wonderful news!' Graham couldn't hide his delight. There were tears in his eyes as he got up and clapped Stephen on the shoulder. 'I can't tell you what this means to me...'

Stephen smiled. 'I think I get the message! You're a scheming, conniving old devil, Graham. If I didn't know that your bypass surgery had been so very necessary, I'd wonder if you hadn't engineered this whole thing just to set me up!'

'I would have done if that was what it took!' Graham admitted without a shred of shame. 'It's always been my dream to have you working alongside me, but I did wonder if it would ever come true. I understood your reasons for not wanting to work here so well, you see.'

Graham paused pensively. Stephen knew that he was thinking back to the old days and felt a lump come to his throat as he realised what a debt he owed this man.

'Still, that's all in the past. Now we have to look forward to the future and make plans accordingly.' Graham sighed. 'I only wish that Alex would be part of this. I still can't get it into my head that she's leaving. I had thought that you and she—' He broke off, looking uncomfortable.

Stephen picked up his cup. What had Graham been going to say—that he'd thought he and Alex would make a good team? There was no chance of that now.

They discussed the new centre after that, bouncing ideas off one another. Stephen found it incredibly stimulating and realised that he had made the right decision. Of course there was still the hurdle of the interview to get over, but he knew in his heart that he would get the job. This was his world, right here. It was where he belonged, where his future lay. It could only have been better if Alex had been sharing it with him.

It had just gone three when he got back to the surgery. Alex's car was in the drive so obviously she'd finished her calls. He let himself in, frowning as he heard a crash from the direction of the office. Dorothy wasn't due for another hour so what was going on in there?

He'd almost reached the door when he heard a voice he didn't recognise. 'Where is it? Tell me or I'll make you sorry!'

His blood ran cold at the menace in the words. Cautiously, he moved the last few steps and peered into the room. Alex was backed up against a filing cabinet and he could tell how scared she was, even though she was doing her best to conceal the fact.

She had every excuse in the world to be afraid, he realised as his gaze moved to the figure standing in front of her. It was obviously male, although a balaclava concealed his features. The knife he was holding made its own statement, however, and Stephen didn't like what it said!

'What's going on here?' he demanded, stepping into the room and immediately drawing the assailant's attention to himself. He knew it was a risky move in such a volatile situation but anything was better than leaving Alex in danger like that.

The man took a few quick steps towards him as Stephen had hoped he would. 'Stay right there!' He raised the knife threateningly and Stephen heard Alex's gasp of dismay. He forced himself not to look at her, afraid that the knifeman's attention would revert to her if he did. If he could keep the man busy by posing the main threat, there was a good chance that she would be safe.

'I asked you what was going on,' he repeated in the same tone of authority, which was guaranteed to arouse a response. If he could provoke the fellow into making a lunge at him there was a chance he could overpower him. Although the man was quite tall he was slightly built, and Stephen was confident he could gain the upper hand if it came to it. However, the knife was a major consideration, he conceded as the man waved it in front of his face.

'You ain't in no position to ask questions, Doc! See this? This is going to ask all the questions round here.'

His voice had risen and Stephen suddenly realised that he was dealing with a youth, not an adult, although whether that made the situation more or less dangerous was hard to tell. He was just weighing it up when another person appeared and came to an abrupt halt as he saw what was happening.

'What're you doin' with that knife, Darren? You said no one was goin' to get hurt!'

'Shut up!' The first youth turned on the newcomer with a snarl of fury, but the damage had been done because Stephen now knew who he was.

'So it's Darren Richardson, is it? I might have known.' He made no attempt to conceal his contempt. 'Not content with injuring innocent little babies, you turn your hand to robbery with violence now.'

'Prove it...any of it!' The boy gave a taunting laugh. 'Anyway, we've wasted enough time. Give me the key to the cupboard—now!'

'I've already told you that I don't know where it is,' Alex piped up. Stephen bit back a groan as the boy's attention swung back to her. He willed her to stay quiet but it seemed the message wasn't getting through because she continued.

'You're wasting your time, Darren. There's no key and there's nothing in the store cupboard of interest to you. Now get out of here!'

'Who do you think you're ordering around?' Darren took a step towards her but Stephen had had enough. He was across the room in a flash, his arm wrapping itself around the boy's neck from behind. He half expected the second youth to join in, but instead he turned tail and ran out of the building.

It was all over in a surprisingly short time. Stephen wrenched the balaclava off the boy's head and smiled grimly. 'I don't think your alibis are going to hold up this time!'

Ignoring Darren's foul-mouthed outburst, he turned to Alex, his gaze softening as he saw how white she was. 'Are you OK?'

'I…I think so. I'll go and phone the police.' She started towards the phone then turned back and there were sparks in her eyes all of a sudden. 'Damn you, Stephen. How dare you put me through that? Don't you realise that you could have been killed, tackling that young thug like that!'

His head started to reel simply because the message she was giving out confused him. Alex cared *that* much that he might have been hurt? 'I…I didn't want him hurting you,' he said roughly, still holding onto a struggling Darren.

Maybe something in his voice gave him away but the anger seemed to drain out of her. She laughed ruefully as her eyes played over his face, and there was an expression in them that made his pulse race. 'This is neither the time nor the place, but it seems to me that you and I need to talk, Stephen. I think we've got our wires crossed somewhere along the way!'

She didn't say anything more, leaving him to wonder what she'd meant. Surely it couldn't be what he imagined…?

He took a deep breath but it didn't help. Was Alex admitting—no, that was too strong—*hinting* that she cared for him? He wasn't sure, but as he waited for the police to arrive the thought was more than enough to blot out all Darren's obscenities!

There was no time to talk before evening surgery began. The police had taken Darren into custody and had needed statements, which had taken up the rest of the afternoon. Stephen felt as though he were living on a knife edge as he saw each patient. The hands of the clock had never moved so slowly before!

Finally the last patient had gone and he was free to find Alex and ask her what she'd meant. He was looking forward to it and dreading it in about equal measures. What if he'd got it all wrong…?

'I said goodnight, Stephen!' Dorothy grinned as he blinked. 'Good job we don't have afternoons like that very often. You were miles away! See you in the morning…both of you.'

Stephen got up as Alex came into the room. He thought he replied to Dorothy's goodbye but he couldn't be sure. Every nerve was humming with tension so that he felt physically ill. It was an effort to wait while Alex closed the door when what he wanted was to bombard her with questions.

'It was busy tonight, wasn't it? I didn't think so many would turn up.' Her tone was bland enough but he had only to look at her face to see evidence of the same tension he was feeling, and suddenly his nervousness evaporated. That Alex—cool, calm and, oh, so composed Alex—should be so uptight filled him with tenderness.

'Neither did I. But isn't it typical?' He came around the desk and took her hands in his, holding them lightly so that she could break free any time she chose to. 'The minute you plan on doing something special, other things get in the way.'

'Yes.' Her voice was husky all of a sudden. He saw her take a deep breath and knew that she was steeling herself to say what she wanted to. Suddenly he knew what it was going to be. It was there in her eyes as she looked at him, in the way she let her hands lie in his so trustingly. Alex loved him. And suddenly he knew that he wanted to make this as easy for her as it suddenly was for him.

'Before you say anything there's something I want to tell you, Alex. I love you.'

There was no mistaking the sincerity in his voice. Alex certainly didn't mistake it, he realised as he saw a dawning joy cross her face. She gave an incoherent murmur as she moved towards him at the same moment he drew her to him. His arms slid around her while he held her as close as he could, feeling the racing of her heart against the pounding of his. It seemed like an omen for the future, their future together.

'I love you, Stephen.'

The whispered confession was swallowed up as he bent to kiss her but it was just as clear for all that. Stephen could hear each word repeating itself inside his head, the most beautiful sounds he'd ever heard! His mouth moved from hers to skim up her cheek, across her brow, down her elegant nose, as though he were absorbing the taste and feel of her, storing away the very essence of this woman he loved with all his heart.

He drew back at last to stare deep into her eyes as he whispered softly, 'I love you, Alex. I love you with my heart and my soul and with every bit of me that's alive.'

'Oh, Stephen, I never thought—' She broke off, laughing as she brushed tears off her cheeks. 'I'm sorry, but these past few weeks have been so awful. Loving you and believing that you cared nothing for me was indescribably painful. I don't know how I've got through each day, to be honest.'

He hugged her close, unable to speak as emotion choked him. He knew how awful she must have felt because he'd felt the same way himself.

It was a moment before he could say anything, and even then it was only after a highly satisfying interlude of kisses which helped unlock the words. 'I think we need to talk this through and see where we went wrong, don't you? But not here.' He shot a meaningful glance around the drab consulting room, hearing her husky laugh.

'I know what you mean! But I don't want to go out any-where, Stephen.' She took a quick breath then looked him squarely in the eye. 'Once we have everything sorted out I want to have you all to myself, not be stuck in the middle of a room full of strangers at some restaurant.'

He took a deep breath because his head was reeling as he understood what she meant. It was his voice which was husky now and tinged with something that brought a wash of colour to her cheeks. 'Then perhaps we'd better move into the sitting-room. It isn't the most romantic place in the world but at least we'll be alone.'

'Sounds perfect to me,' she agreed, leading the way. It took some time to traverse the short distance, mainly because they stopped several times on the way to kiss. Stephen was glad when he was able to plop down onto the sofa because he wasn't sure his legs would have supported him much longer!

'Come here.' He held his hand out, smiling as Alex came and sat beside him. He drew her head onto his shoulder, letting his fingers stroke her cheek. Frankly, he would have been happy to sit there and do just that for the next week, but there were questions to be asked and answers to be given.

He let his hand come to rest on the rounded end of her shoulder. 'Do you want to go first or shall I?'

'I will.' She brushed a kiss along his jaw, smiling as she felt the shiver that danced beneath his skin. There was a faintly smug note in her voice as she continued but Stephen forgave her for it, mainly because he was planning on feeling smug himself in a very short time!

'I suppose the best place to start is at the beginning, when Graham told me that he was going to ask you to come here and cover for him while he was in hospital,' she said quietly.

'I don't need to ask how you felt about that!' Stephen said wryly, and heard her laugh.

'Hmm, well, at the time I thought the frosty welcome was justified!' She sighed, taking his hand to link her fingers through his. 'Graham had told me so much about you, you see.

About your work and how successful you were. I'd already summed you up before you got here, as I've explained before, but it threw me when I realised you weren't what I'd expected.'

Stephen grinned as he raised her hand to his lips and covered her palm with kisses. 'Remind me to tell you about the picture I'd formed of you some time!'

'I'm not sure I want to know!' she retorted laughingly. 'Anyway, to get back to my confession, I had you down as someone who was only interested in money and status and little else. That was why you'd gone into private practice, I assumed, and why you never took time out to visit Graham, even when he was so desperately ill.'

'I had no idea how bad he was,' Stephen asserted quietly. 'Every time I asked him how he was he brushed it aside, although that isn't any excuse—'

'It's OK, darling,' she put in quickly, hearing the pain in his voice. 'Graham confessed how underhanded he'd been, telling you that his angina wasn't causing him any problems. He hadn't wanted to worry you, you see. He knew how upset you'd be.'

'At least I could have helped him out sooner!' He took a deep breath then smiled ruefully. 'Sorry, but I could wring his neck for putting himself at risk the way he did. He's a stubborn old fool and I've told him that.'

'You and me both!' Alex laughed. 'Anyway, once you were actually here I found that my impression of you didn't gel with the reality. The way you treated the patients, taking such an interest in their lives as well as their illnesses, the way you…you *cared*. But it was when you told me about your childhood that I finally realised the Stephen Spencer I'd imagined didn't exist and in his place was a man whom I could very easily learn to love.'

'Oh, Alex!' He drew her to him, kissing her until they were both breathless. He gave a shaky laugh as he cupped her face between his hands. 'I thought you'd hate me even more when you learned about my past. It's a world away from the life you knew so I was sure your opinion of me would only deteriorate further.'

'No! Oh, Stephen, it never crossed my mind! It had just the opposite effect, in fact. Hearing how you had overcome such huge odds to get where you are, it was humbling. I realised that I had no right to sit in judgement on you and that if you decided not to go after the directorship of the health centre it was understandable. I certainly wouldn't have thought any less of you for it, even though I still believe you'd be making a mistake.'

'That's good to hear, but I told Graham today that I'm interested in the post.' He smoothed his thumb across her lips, almost groaning out loud when they immediately parted. 'I intend to stay here and work because it's where I want to be, Alex. I can make a valuable contribution and you helped me see that is more important than status or money. I think I'd half reached that conclusion myself, but you brought home to me what I was lacking in my life. I...I only hope that you'll be here to share this new venture with me.'

She must have heard the uncertainty in his voice, which even recent revelations hadn't quite erased. 'Of course I'll be here! I'm not going anywhere without you, darling!'

'Not even to Africa with Simon?' he teased, reassured by her vehemence.

'No.' She rolled her eyes comically. 'That was just something I thought up for Graham's benefit, to explain why I was leaving the practice. I might even have gone through with it— who knows? But I never wanted to leave, believe me. I...I just knew it would be too painful, working here, if you did decide to stay on when you'd made it plain that you didn't feel anything for me.'

'When did I do that?' He couldn't hide his astonishment and he saw her frown.

'That night after we'd taken Danny to the river when things got a little...well, fraught between us.'

'Fraught? That's one way to describe it,' he said drily, and saw her blush. 'I wanted to make love to you so much that night, Alex! But you turned round and told me that you'd only ever sleep with the man you loved. You made it plain that wasn't me so I managed to stop myself telling you how crazy I was about you.'

'Not you? But I was trying to tell you that it *was* you I was in love with! That was the only reason I'd think of going to bed with you. I was hoping and praying that you would tell me that you felt the same way!'

'You were? But I thought...' He groaned. 'Talk about getting our wires crossed, indeed. What idiots we are!'

'Uh-huh. But there's an easy way to resolve this, isn't there?' She stood up and held out her hand. 'Let's carry on where we left off that night. Think you can remember where we'd got to?'

'Oh, I think so. Although you may need to refresh my memory about some of the finer points.' He stood up as well, pulling her to him so fast that she gasped. Her lips were just as eager as his when he kissed her, however, telling him that her memory of that night was as clear as his...

He rested his forehead against hers, putting off the moment a little longer. 'You are sure this is what you want, Alex? Absolutely and completely—?'

'Certain,' she put in softly. 'Now, are we going to waste time debating it or what?'

He swung her up into his arms, laughing into her eyes as his heart swelled with love. 'Oh, most definitely ''or what''!'

EPILOGUE

'DR SPENCER...the hospital is on the phone. It's time!'

'Tell them I'll be straight there, Debbie!' Stephen turned to Graham, his face reflecting myriad emotions. 'Will you be all right here? I hate to let you down but...'

'But Alex needs you!' Graham clapped him on the shoulder. 'Go on, get out of here. I think we can just about hold the place together without you!'

Everyone laughed and even Stephen had to smile as he headed for the door at a run. With three full-time doctors apart from himself, plus Graham in a part-time capacity, the new health centre was certainly adequately staffed. It would manage perfectly well without him for once!

The full complement of staff was now in place and included two practice nurses, a midwife and a health visitor. He'd had to fight to get what he wanted but the health authority had capitulated in the end. Dorothy was in charge of Reception and was training two new receptionists to her exacting standards. Debbie Francis was one of them and was proving invaluable. Things were working out very nicely indeed. Fingers crossed that the next few hours went so well!

He broke all records getting to the hospital, then wasted valuable minutes hunting for a parking space. He was out of breath by the time he made it to the maternity unit so that he could barely puff out the necessary introduction. 'I'm Stephen Spencer. You have my wife...'

'Just in time, Dr Spencer. Another few minutes and you'd have missed it.' Handing him a green overall, the midwife quickly led the way to the delivery room. 'He's here at last, Alex. Take it from me, doctors are always the last to arrive when it's their child being born!'

'So long as he got here—' Alex broke off on a gasp as Stephen hurried into the room, hastily fastening the overall. It needed only a glance to tell him that the midwife hadn't been exaggerating and that the baby was about to be born.

The next few minutes passed in a daze so that Stephen could hardly believe it when the baby was placed in his arms. 'A girl?' he muttered, tears filling his eyes as he saw the precious new life that he and Alex had created. He turned to her, not even trying to hide how he felt.

'We have a daughter, Alex…a little girl…' He couldn't go on as the enormity of it all hit him.

'I had a feeling it was going to be a girl,' she said huskily, holding out her arms for the baby. She stroked the tiny crumpled cheek with a gentle finger, her own eyes misting with tears. 'She's beautiful, Stephen, isn't she?'

'Just like her mother.' He bent and kissed her tenderly then grinned. 'Wait till everyone hears it's a girl. Graham had a bet with Dorothy that it would be a boy, you know.'

'Probably because he was hoping for a playmate for Tim,' Alex said with a laugh. Everyone had been thrilled when Graham and Meg had married and then, out of the blue, produced their son.

'Probably,' Stephen agreed, stroking the baby's cheek to convince himself that she was real.

He and Alex had been so happy since they'd married twelve months before. He hadn't thought that things could have got any better, but suddenly he knew he'd been wrong. To have Alex and their child—that was more than any man could dream of having in one lifetime!

His tone was even huskier as he realised how lucky he was. 'So, have we settled on a name for her? I was so sure it would be a boy.'

Alex smiled. 'Shouldn't count your chickens, should you? But, yes, I know what I'd like to call her, if you're agreeable that is—Hannah, after your mother.'

'Are you sure?' He was choked with emotion and had to dash the tears from his eyes. 'She would have been so proud.'

'I know.' Alex's eyes shimmered before she gave a rueful laugh. 'There's just one drawback. I think for the sake of peace we'll have to add Louise as her second name. I never thought I'd see the day when my mother turned into the proverbial doting granny, but she's been so excited!'

Stephen laughed. He slid his finger under the baby's chin as she gave a huge yawn. 'Is that all very boring for you, poppet?' He smiled as the baby pulled a funny little face. 'I think that was a yes, don't you? Hannah Louise Spencer—quite a mouthful for such a tiny scrap, but I like it.'

'Good.' Alex smiled up at him with her heart in her eyes. 'I love you, Stephen Spencer. Have I told you that lately?'

'Oh, not for at least three hours. Time you told me again…'

He bent and kissed her, letting his mouth say everything that needed to be said. Now his world was complete and what he had was greater than any amount of riches.

MILLS & BOON®

Makes any time special™

Mills & Boon publish 29 new titles every month. Select from...

Modern Romance™   Tender Romance™

Sensual Romance™

Medical Romance™   Historical Romance™

MAT2

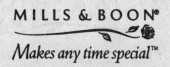

books and a surprise gift!

We would like to take this opportunity to thank you for reading this Mills & Boon® book by offering you the chance to take FOUR more specially selected titles from the Medical Romance™ series absolutely FREE! We're also making this offer to introduce you to the benefits of the Reader Service™—

- ★ FREE home delivery
- ★ FREE gifts and competitions
- ★ FREE monthly Newsletter
- ★ Exclusive Reader Service discounts
- ★ Books available before they're in the shops

Accepting these FREE books and gift places you under no obligation to buy, you may cancel at any time, even after receiving your free shipment. Simply complete your details below and return the entire page to the address below. *You don't even need a stamp!*

YES! Please send me 4 free Medical Romance books and a surprise gift. I understand that unless you hear from me, I will receive 6 superb new titles every month for just £2.40 each, postage and packing free. I am under no obligation to purchase any books and may cancel my subscription at any time. The free books and gift will be mine to keep in any case.

M0ZEA

Ms/Mrs/Miss/Mr ....Initials......................................
BLOCK CAPITALS PLEASE

Surname ....

Address ....

....

....Postcode................................

Send this whole page to:
UK: FREEPOST CN81, Croydon, CR9 3WZ
EIRE: PO Box 4546, Kilcock, County Kildare (stamp required)